This book is dedicated to Elvira Phoenix Martin, for without whom, it would still be a short story locked away in my computer. Thank you for believing in me.

And to Phil, thank you for keeping the park gates open.

Simple Pleasures

Copyright © 2012 by Natasha D.T. Simmons

Simple Pleasures

By: Natasha Simmons

Prologue

The unusually large crowd at the campus coffee shop and the fact that it looked as if the day had been dipped in a bucket of gray paint did not dampen Alexandra Wyatt's mood. Since starting her freshman year at Loyola University in New Orleans eight years ago, she'd become accustomed to dark clouds that often threatened the spring sky.

The brass band hired for the special "after-commencement" celebration had been forced to move inside due to the ominous weather. She was thrilled to find a table outside in the garden, away from the noisy throng, ominous sky or not. She sat at the small wrought-iron table for two, feeling strange and disencumbered. There were no heavy books or computer to burden her today. Toying with her coffee cup, not really needing the boost of caffeine, she looked around, thinking that the vivid pink of the newly-bloomed azaleas seemed oddly out of place against the drab background of the sky. She sighed and thought about how proud her father would have been of her.

"You know, I think I may have to see a doctor."

She was still sitting quietly at her table, smiling with the triumph of getting to this very important moment in her life, so it took Alex a few seconds to realize that the deep, rich tones were directed at her.

"Wha...I'm sorry, are you talking to me?" she said, looking up from her table, rather annoyed that this voice had distracted her from her own private celebration.

Her breath was momentarily stolen from her as she looked up into eyes and a smile so compellingly warm and kind that she was sure she could see embers smoldering. When her brain finally caught up with her ears, she realized the man was saying something about seeing his doctor.

"Your doctor?" she stuttered, then realized he looked vaguely familiar. Had she taken a class with him? Maybe she'd seen him in the sports bar where she was a part-time bartender.

"Yeah, I may need to see my doctor. By the way, that's some grip you have. Do you have a license for that hug of yours?"

For a moment, she was disoriented. He went on to congratulate her on her degree, as he did all the students he saw still wearing their gowns after the graduation ceremony. As he spoke, she realized he was the professor she had hugged so fiercely after she received her diploma.

She was beginning to turn crimson in remembrance, and he found himself amused by her reaction. Most of the female students on campus were not shy at all and practically threw themselves at him. Being a professor, he was constantly aware of it. He kept his distance and avoided anything that would even slightly be a potential scandal. But this beautiful creature had him mesmerized, and she seemed totally oblivious to the effect she had on him. This should be interesting, he thought.

"A license? Well, actually, I'm board-certified in hugging." The seriousness of her face did not distract from the mischief in her eyes.

"And does this certification have limitations in just the giving, or does it allow for receiving as well?"

Oh my, what had she gotten herself into? She didn't know why she had started this thread of conversation, but thought she might as well roll with it.

"Both," she said. "At my discretion, of course."

"I see." Joshua remembered how she had fit into his arms perfectly. "And may I also ask if you carry some sort of malpractice insurance?"

Alex cocked her head to the side and lifted an eyebrow as she looked up at him.

"Will there be a lawsuit?"

"Maybe," he whispered, seeming to thoroughly enjoy himself.

She usually wasn't so free to encourage conversation, especially anything so close to being considered witty banter. She generally kept a protective shield around her. Men were distractions that she couldn't afford to indulge in. But today, she'd wished for someone to share her joy. This stranger would have to do.

"Will it help if I apologized? I'm sorry, but you *are* in the line of fire up there on that stage. You never know how someone may react."

"I'll accept your apology, Ms. Wyatt, if you allow me to join you." His voice was like a warm blanket in winter.

"Do you remember all the names of the graduates, Professor?

"Not usually, but it is hard to forget a heartfelt embrace like yours. And the name is Joshua."

"Well, Joshua, if you forever forego any further legal action against me…. I'm Alexandra…Alex," she said with only a hint of a smile.

"Spoken like a true lawyer," he said as he took a seat at the small table.

She wished she could just close her eyes and listen to the sound of his voice. "Not yet, but soon. To seal the deal, why don't you let me buy you a cup of coffee?"

What was she doing? Buying a man a cup of coffee? She had never done that before. She had never had time for such things. Today, though, she just wanted to relax and have a regular conversation.

"We have a deal."

He reached out a hand to make it official. His hand felt strong enough to protect and gentle enough to entice her body to do its will. Goodness. Alexandra was slightly shocked at the course her thoughts had taken.

"What's your pleasure?" she said, bringing her mind back on track and using a phrase she often used at the bar, only this time referring to the coffee she'd offered.

"A quiet little place that's not very known where you can get the best homemade pasta in the city; a glass of my favorite red wine; taking the time to start and finish a really great book; calm seas with no shore in sight; glancing at the clock and finding out I still have three more hours to sleep. My pleasure is to always have that smile of yours staring back at me."

She said nothing for almost a whole minute. His deep, brown eyes bore into her and whispered something sweet to her soul.

"Okay," was all she said.

Chapter 1

The rain was coming down so hard; she couldn't quite hear what he was saying. She leaned in to ask him to repeat it, because his eyes held such conviction as he spoke. With practiced ease, he gently cupped her face and leaned in to whisper in her ear. He was so close to her face, the smell of his aftershave made her toes tingle. She heard the chocolate vibrations of his voice, but could not make out what he was saying to her. She pressed her head closer, still unable to hear him, but she was too lost in the silky feeling of his beard to find the key to unlock her voice.

"Is that okay with you?" she thought she heard him say, but she still couldn't speak. His lips were so close to hers; she only had to shift her head slightly to discover if he tasted as delicious as he sounded. Sweeping her tongue across her bottom lip in anticipation of something so rich and indulgent; she could hardly remember to breathe.

Alex woke, but refused to open her eyes, hoping it was actually rain she heard, but fearing it was only the shower from her neighbor's apartment. With disappointment and annoyance, she quickly realized it was the latter when the single-man chorus began his tuneless rendition of Madonna's *Like a Virgin*. Trying desperately not to get a visual of a grown man in the shower pretending to be Madonna, she tried recapturing her dream. It had been so vivid that her heart was still racing, and she could still smell him. As she lay there with her eyes closed, she resigned herself to the fact that it was indeed a dream, and she felt a bit disappointed that she didn't get to taste him…

Taste him? What was she thinking? She needed to get up, to get ready for class, but her body was giving in to her exhaustion. Alex had a mind to sleep in today, though she couldn't shake the feeling that there was something important she needed to be doing.

What a dream! The intoxicating aroma she sensed was still romancing her nose. She couldn't remember the last time a dream had remained so vivid after waking, or even dreaming about a man, for that matter.

Her eyes flew open and she saw it. She didn't have class; it was Sunday and yesterday had been her graduation. School was finally over. Her diploma sat proudly as proof of all the sacrifices she'd made over the past eight years, one of them being men. Keeping herself free from any distractions had been important to getting her law degree.

The shower next door had stopped, and shortly after, the singing as well. Richard, her next-door neighbor, should be leaving for work soon, so she could actually try sleeping in with no disturbances. His apartment had been empty when she moved in, so it wasn't until Richard arrived and had company over, that she realized how paper-thin the walls were.

He had tried, without success, to get her to keep him company, but luckily it had only taken one confrontation with her for him to permanently scratch Alexandra off his "to-do" list. Her exact words had been, "Richard, I have no inclination whatsoever to join the airhead-parade that constantly passes my apartment seeking to turn your entranceway into a revolving door of come in, giggle, moan, shout, and get out." His face had gone through the gamut of emotions from shock to anger, disbelief and finally indifference. It had been like watching a kid put different faces on a blank cartoon head.

Her eyes closed again and she could smell Joshua's scent floating towards her brain, just as she was drifting off to sleep. Maybe she could conjure up the dream again. She rolled over and snuggled into her pillow.

"Damn it," she thought. The scent was gone. She rolled back to the other side, and there it was again. She let out a relaxing breath and snuggled into her pillow. Something wasn't right. Her eyes were closed, but she was awake and could still smell his cologne. Noises from next door invaded her space, but as far as she could remember, none of the fumes from the love concoctions that Richard brewed had ever wafted in. She sat up and opened her eyes, scanning the room. She needed a cup of coffee.

Coffee! It all came back to her. The coffee and conversation she had shared with the professor. She hadn't dreamed those things he'd said to her. His pleasures. She thought about the things he had said and she remembered how the words flowed around her, pulling her into each sound and vibration of his voice. She remembered every syllable he had spoken and how his mouth moved when he uttered them. Momentarily hypnotized, she remembered him saying he wanted to always have that smile of hers staring back at him. The next thing she remembered was suddenly being drenched by the sudden emergence of a rainstorm. Joshua had handed his jacket to her as they both ran for cover.

His jacket! She looked around the room and there it was, lying on the floor right next to her bed. She reached down to pick up the supple, black, leather garment and with the gentleness of lifting a newborn, she brought the jacket to her face and his scent released bolts of electricity through her middle. She could not understand what was going on with her. She worked at an upscale sports bar that was frequented by drop-dead, good-looking brothers. The kind that could make your panties moist just by looking at them, she'd heard the ladies say, though she wasn't sure what they meant. So she couldn't understand why she was reacting the way she was towards Joshua. For goodness sakes, she didn't even know his last name.

What still lingered in her mind was his delicious voice, just made you want to lick and nibble a piece of rich, dark chocolate. She inhaled the fragrance that was the epitome of masculinity and her heart began to flutter, though Alex wasn't sure if the flutter was from excitement or nervousness.

The sign read: "Office of Dr. Joshua Phoenix." Joshua slid the nameplate out of the wall slot and placed it in the box along with some articles he'd cleared off his desk. He had taught Business Ethics at Loyola for the past seven years. He'd only planned to teach there for a few years as a favor to his old friend and mentor, Paul Bash, who happened to be the dean of students, but Hurricane Katrina's rage had changed his plans, along with those of countless others. He felt obligated to extend his tenure until the school was well on its feet after the storm. Sustaining minimal damage, the school was able to resume classes more quickly than most of the universities in the area. Joshua had not wanted to add the burden of looking for someone to replace him on top of dealing with the aftermath of the storm.

Joshua was so excited to start a new adventure; though he loved teaching, it was not his true passion. All he'd thought about this last semester was getting through the commencement ceremony and completing the packing of his office so that he could board his new sailboat and surrender to the adventures that awaited him. It was finally completed. He saw to it that every last detail was perfection. Joshua would leave all the sadness and hurts of his life and cling to the only thing he knew would be worthy of his love, the ocean.

But now, instead of dreaming of his nautical quests, as he had for the past several months, all he could focus on was Alexandra Wyatt's enchanting smile. He remembered every detail about her. Her brown hair was twisted into a thick bun that perched above her starched white collar. He could just envision stripping that bun of the pins that held it taut and having her hair tumble down in waves that rested over her breasts. The black robe she wore hid the figure that he imagined was perfect underneath it. Her round, honey-bronze face was smooth and flawless and had an appearance of softness that could only belong to a heavenly cherub.

But it was her smile that stole the show. When he'd first walked up to her, she was sitting there, smiling with the corners of her mouth turned up slightly, as if she were reliving a pleasant memory, but when she parted her full, luscious lips and gave an unabridged smile, oh, my. Joshua's world suddenly stopped and he became captivated by her sheer beauty. She had dimples that transformed into two delectable black hollows that he wanted to get lost in. Alexandra Wyatt was simply an angel on earth.

Joshua couldn't understand why he was so taken with Alex. Surely he'd seen beautiful women before, but he had to admit none of them could hold a candle to Alex. He couldn't believe he had said those things to her, but he knew at that moment, nothing else mattered but that smile of hers.

She'd said, "Okay," but to what? The rain interrupted them and then she was gone, with his jacket as a shield from the downpour. He heard her yell back to him that she would get the jacket back first thing Monday morning. It was Monday and the service he had hired to move his belongings would be there soon and afterwards there would be no reason to hang around his office. *You idiot,* he thought. He hadn't even given her his last name. He was so humored by their conversation, he never got around to really introducing himself properly.

How would he see her again? He dropped into his chair and tried to conjure up a reason to give admin to provide him her address or phone number. He ripped the tape off one the boxes and tore through it, looking for his campus directory. Joshua stopped and looked towards the door, thinking maybe one of his colleagues had her on their rolls. Nah, that wouldn't work. They would want to know why he needed it and start making all sorts of speculations.

"Hey, man, I thought you were packing, not unpacking. What are you looking for?" The voice startled Joshua and he accidentally knocked the box over when he spun around. It was David Breaux from the office next door.

"What's up, Dave? I didn't think you were here today," Joshua said, sounding a little agitated. David narrowed his eyes at his friend.

"You okay, Josh? You look like you just got caught with your hand in the cookie jar." "Yea, umm, I was just looking for my campus directory," Joshua said.

David wondered why Josh seemed so unglued. He was usually calm and confident. Nothing ever seemed to ruffle his feathers. David's curiosity was piqued at what was going on with Mr. Calm and Collected.

"I thought you were eager to close up shop and put this school behind you. Aren't you ready to hit the open seas that will take you to unknown shores, hopefully full of scantily-clad temptations of the best kind?" he asked with twinge of envy.

"I am, man. I just need to tie up some loose ends before I…"

Joshua could not utter another word. His gaze was transfixed by the image in his doorway. For the life of him, he could not make his brain remember how to speak or close his mouth.

David furrowed his brow and turned to see what seemed to have Joshua stuck on pause.

Chapter 2

Alex wasn't sure if she had come to the right office because there was no name on the door, but the building directory had this room number listed for Dr. Joshua Phoenix. She had gotten his last name from the commencement program. The program also stated he was one of the Business Ethics professors, which made him much easier to find. She was about to turn around, thinking she must have looked at the wrong room number, when she heard a voice that made her soul stir. It was him. Her hands suddenly felt damp and it had nothing to do with the coffee she held.

Did women do things like this? Did they just show up unannounced? What if he got the wrong impression from her?

She'd always been annoyed by the groups of female students wasting their study time, laughing and talking in the courtyard as she emerged alone from the library, laden with books. She never regretted one moment of her study time. Every hour and sleepless night was dedicated to the memory of her father. She had been determined to become the woman he dreamed her to be, but today, she envied those girls in the courtyard. They would know the answers to her questions.

What was wrong with her? She was just returning his jacket and bringing him the cup of coffee that she had promised and never got around to buying because of the rain. She took a deep breath, stepped in the doorway, and there he was. He seemed bigger than life. He had to be about six-four and towered over her mere five-foot frame. If any man could be called beautiful, it would have to be him. With skin the color of rich chocolate, he was the poster child for tall, dark and "damn could he be any finer". His smooth black eyebrows seemed to be tailor-made just for his face and perfectly framed a pair of the most piercing brown eyes she'd ever seen. His hair was curly, black, and made you wonder how such a dark brother came upon having such semi-silky locks. It would be just long enough to run your fingers through as he lay on bare breasts after a bout of lovemaking.

Her breasts began to tingle at the thought. *Where did that thought come from? Get yourself together girl. You're behaving like a wanton floozy.* She suddenly realized he was staring at her with his mouth open, as if she had caught him mid-sentence.

David looked from Joshua to the lady in the doorway and neither of them seemed to notice he was in the room. *This must be the reason Josh was coming unglued earlier,* he thought. And he could definitely see why. Whoever she was, she was a knockout.

"Ahem," David cleared his throat to bring them both back to reality.

Joshua seemed to find his voice and quickly stood.

"Alex, how are you? I see you made it through the rainstorm okay. I was hoping you made it home before the streets began to flood. You know, it doesn't take much for the streets here in New Orleans to fill up with water and make driving impossible. Did you encounter any trouble?"

David lifted an eyebrow towards Joshua. This had to be the first time he'd heard Josh ramble. He hadn't giving the poor woman a chance to speak.

"I'm sorry my colleague is being so rude," David broke in.

"I'm David Breaux," he said as he extended a hand to her.

"Alexandra Wyatt, nice to meet you," she said with a firm shake. She turned back to Joshua, holding the cup of coffee and his jacket draped across her arm in the drycleaner's bag.

"And to answer your questions, Professor Phoenix, I am fine and made it home before the streets began to flood. I live only a few blocks from here. Thank you for the use of your jacket. I took the liberty of having it cleaned for you and hope the rain did not damage it."

"Please, Alex, call me Joshua."

Joshua then turned to David, who seemed to be rather enjoying the little scene taking place before him and appreciating the view a little too much.

"David, thanks for dropping by. I'll poke my head in your office before I leave this afternoon."

Before Joshua could usher him through the door, David turned and said, "It was a pleasure meeting you, Ms. Wyatt." He turned back to Joshua and gave him a sly grin and a wink as he walked back to his office.

Joshua closed the office door, not understanding why his heart seemed to be in overdrive. He couldn't believe she was actually standing here in his office. When he turned, he saw Alex looking around for a place to hang the jacket.

"I'll take that. Thank you. It wasn't necessary for you to go through the trouble of having it cleaned," he said as he sat the jacket on a box.

"No, thank you. It was very kind and noble of you to give your jacket to a stranger. I just wanted to show my appreciation. Oh, and by the way, here is the cup of coffee we agreed on for the settlement," she said, handing him the cup.

"Thank you," he said, not wanting anything to be settled between them. "Again, you didn't have to go to any trouble, but it is good to see you," he added huskily.

Alex glanced around the room and noticed all the boxes.

"Do you mind if I ask you something?" she finally turned to say.

"Oh, you're wondering about all the boxes? Well…" he said.

"Well yes," she said, not waiting for him to finish, "but that's not what I wanted to know."

"Oh? What would you like to know?"

"Are you some kind of knight in shining armor or something?" she asked, as seriously as she could.

"Excuse me? I'm not following you."

"I mean, we're in New Orleans… in May. Why on earth would you be carrying a leather jacket around, if not waiting to rescue a damsel in distress?"

He just stood there staring at her, not at all prepared for the question she'd asked. He sat back on his desk and let out a deep, throaty laugh. She was absolutely breathtaking, standing there in his office with her hand on her hip, waiting for a response that she seemed to think was logical enough. And in fact it was. No one in their right mind *would* be walking around with a leather jacket in this heat.

But a damsel in distress, she was not. Standing there in a yellow suit that fitted her to a tee, she was the epitome of confidence. Her skirt was a few inches above her knees and showed off a pair of shapely, golden legs. Her hair she still wore pulled back in a severe bun, giving her the appearance of someone who was all work and no play. But the conversation they had on Saturday had indicated there was a vixen in her that was dying to come out. And he prayed to the gods that he could be around when it did. He realized suddenly that she was starting to get a little uncomfortable with his close scrutiny of her and decided he'd better answer her question.

"Please Alex, have a seat. I didn't mean to seem so rude," he said, directing her to a chair.

Rude was the last thing she was thinking, he seemed. He seemed downright decadent to her. She had to get herself together. For the life of her, she couldn't understand why ever since meeting Joshua, her thoughts had become simply scandalous.

"No, thanks, I have a meeting I am on my way to."

Joshua was a bit disappointed at the thought of her leaving so soon. He would be flying to New England in the morning to see the end product of a dream come true. He realized, then, she was still waiting there with that hand on her hip and one eyebrow arched.

"To answer your questions, no, I am far from being a knight in shining armor and there is a good

20

reason why I was carrying a leather jacket in New Orleans in May."

"Which is?" she asked.

"As you can see, I have packed my office. The jacket has been here since winter and I decided to take it home on Saturday to make sure it gets packed with my luggage. I will be leaving in the morning to fly to my newly-built sailboat. The jacket, I am sure I will need in the evenings sometimes."

"I see…well, thanks again. I wish you a safe flight and calm seas."

She only wished she felt calm. Her heart was banging out of her chest. She was sure he could hear it. She was rather disappointed that he was leaving, but it was just as well. He looked too damned good, leaning against that desk just as casual as he pleased. When she saw him after the graduation, he had looked like someone off the cover of *GQ* in his suit. Just as sexy as he could be. But today, standing here casually in his office, wearing a pair of jeans and a polo shirt, sexiness screamed from his pores. She needed to turn her thoughts in another direction, get her head on straight to decide where she wanted to practice and to study for the bar exam. Alex turned to leave.

Joshua could have sworn he saw disappointment in her eyes when he said he was leaving, but it could have been wishful thinking on his part. Wishful thinking? What was going on with him? He didn't have time for this. Hadn't he learned his lesson with Victoria?

Victoria Johnson was the woman he had intended to marry, but she soon had realized her career was more important than a husband and a family. Now she was a rising star in the financial world. Victoria was known for her cold persona and her "grab them by the balls" business tactics. Put simply, she was ruthless. He'd dated her during college. She was beautiful and everything his parents wanted in a wife for him. Her parents were in the same social circles as his and he had fallen in love with her when he escorted her to the cotillion at the end of her senior year of high school.

They had dated all through college and everyone was sure they would marry when they finished grad school. He was too, but when she was offered her dream job on Wall Street, she basically laughed in his face when he presented the ring to her. She didn't want to be tied down to a husband and definitely didn't want to be saddled with any kids. Joshua was devastated. He had invested eight years of his life in this woman, and she just shut him down without batting an eye. He knew then that he would not be able to get serious about another career-minded businesswoman again.

Alexandra Wyatt had finished at the top of her class, and he was sure already had offers to some of the most influential law firms in the country. She was smart and appeared to be savvy as well, but there was warmth about her that spoke to him. He couldn't let that fool him. She was focused on her career. But, still, that didn't mean he couldn't take her to dinner before he left in the morning.

"Alex," he called out to her.

She turned, "Yes?"

"I'm sorry, Alex, but our verbal agreement had the stipulation of me *joining* you for a cup of coffee, so this won't do," he said, pointing to the cup in his hand.

She turned to fully face him then, with that eyebrow easing up on the forehead he was quickly becoming addicted to.

"I beg your pardon?" she said.

"Ms. Wyatt, you don't have to beg me for anything," he said with a smile.

Alex was about to fire off some words at him but his statement took the wind out of her sails. She just stared at him, trying to pull her thoughts together. He was knocking her off balance and she was sure the temperature had risen twenty degrees. This was her thing. The snappy comeback was what she was known for. She was never caught off guard, but from the moment she had met Joshua Phoenix, she had turned into a bumbling idiot.

"It's my last night here, and you may not have the opportunity to settle out of court. I may just have to sue you."

"Oh, really?"

"Yes, really."

"Well, Dr. Phoenix, unfortunately a courtroom is not in your future. Mine, yes, but yours…"

He cut her off. "My what?" he whispered, as he took a step towards her.

"Your …." She was getting lost in those eyes of his and had momentarily forgotten what they were discussing. The phone rang and brought her out of the fog she was drifting into. Joshua turned to answer it. She was going to have to check her law books because there had to be a law in the state of Louisiana that prevented any man from exuding so much sex appeal. And it did not help that he was wearing the same cologne that had triggered so many tacky thoughts since she'd met him.

He turned then and smiled. She was almost a goner but pulled herself together. She stood as tall as her five feet would take her and looked him squarely in the eyes. "As I was saying, Dr. Phoenix…"

"Please, call me Joshua"

"As I was saying, Joshua, there is no courtroom in your future, not with me, anyway. The cup of coffee you hold in your hands signifies the acceptance of our verbal agreement, so case closed. Again, you have a safe trip, and thanks for your chivalry."

She smiled sweetly, turned and walked out the door. She didn't even bother to shake his hand.

Joshua leaned back on his desk, took a sip of coffee, and thought about where he would take her to dinner.

Chapter 3

Alex sat at her kitchen table, staring at the two envelopes lying there. The brief meeting with Preston Fontenot, her father's longtime attorney, was a stark reminder of how alone she was in this world. He had congratulated her for receiving her graduate degree and had given her the envelopes, one of which he'd waited eight years to give. For it had been eight years since her father had lost his battle with cancer.

Carl Wyatt had been one of the leading environmental lawyers in the state of Louisiana and it was his dream for Alexandra to follow in his footsteps. They were to be Wyatt and Wyatt, Attorneys at Law, a formidable team. Alexandra's father meant the world to her. He was mother, father and her best friend.

Though Alex was only four at the time, she would never forget when her dad told her that Mamma had gone to heaven. It was the only time she remembered ever seeing her father cry. He'd kept saying, "What am I going to do without her?" Alex crawled into his lap, hugged him, and whispered, "Don't cry, Daddy. God must have had something special for Mamma to do in heaven. She left me here to take care of you. I love you, Daddy."

"You know, you really are something special, Alexandra."

"That's because Mamma was special and you always said I was just like her."

Carl Wyatt had hugged his daughter tight and thanked God for her.

Alex picked up one of the envelopes and passed her fingers over the handwriting she knew so well. She couldn't help the lone tear that made its way down her cheek. She smiled, in spite of the tightness in her throat. Her father had the worst handwriting of anyone she knew. When had he written this? And why had she not been given it sooner? She opened the envelope and was thankful her father had the forethought to have the letter typed, by Sophie, his longtime secretary, no doubt.

My dearest Alexandra,

Pride swells in me for the woman I know you have become. Carl was instructed to give this letter to you upon the completion of your law degree. There is not a doubt in my mind you will not receive this letter. Everything I've known you to have set out to do, you have accomplished. No doubt there have been many grand adventures in your life thus far. I am also sure, my beautiful daughter, you have broken several hearts along the way. Oh, how I wish I could be there to see you rejoice in your accomplishments with your friends, but I am not sad and neither should you be. I will live in the wonderful memories we've shared. I know my dear, at this special moment in your life come great feelings of culmination, but with them there are choices that lie ahead on your continued journey. Have no fear, Sweetheart, if I were with you, I would support any decision you make in regards to your future or anything else in your life. Even as a child, you were wiser than your years and you've always made choices that were best for you.

My wish for you is to not have any financial burdens that may hinder you from following your heart. In this business it is easy to be lured to the dark side of the law because the money is right. I want you to work for something you are passionate about. For when you are passionate about a cause, your energy is fueled by something that has no price. And that, my dear, is what makes us successful and stand out from the rest. Your college trust fund has carried you thus far, but the other envelope Preston has given you will carry you the rest of the way. Take care, my dear. Please know that my love for you did not end with my last breath. I am with you always, Allie. Remember when you follow your heart in life, it will never lead you astray. I am so proud of you.

Love always,

Daddy

Allie. He'd called her Allie. Alex could not stop the tears that flooded her. She cried for the father she'd lost. She cried for the stark loneliness that enveloped her. She cried for how wrong he was. There were no friends to share her success, there were no broken hearts, and there were no grand adventures or any of the things her father had wished for. He had been everything to her, and when he died she replaced her emptiness with school. Her only outlet away from school for the past eight years had been her part-time job at the sports bar and restaurant. She'd only started working there because her school counselor suggested she needed something else in her life besides school or she would burn out.

She had seen the advertisement in the *Times-Picayune* three years ago and called. She didn't have any experience working anywhere and definitely didn't know anything about working in a bar, but she showed up to the interview anyway. The manager got one look at her and knew she would be great for business. Her boss was great and made sure none of the men harassed her. Alex was trained as a waitress and after a year, was trained to work behind the bar. She made a killing in tips. All the men tried to hit on her at first, but soon found out it was a no-win situation. It did not go unnoticed to the manager that business was better on the nights she worked. Even if they knew there was no chance of getting a date with her, they came just for the rare occasion she might grant them one of her famous smiles. They were rare, but when you got one, your life was perfect, if only for a moment. Alex had come to love her job and had managed the bar on several occasions when her manager was unable to come in.

Alex now cried until there were no tears left. She thought of her father and knew he would not have wanted her to cry. He'd hated to see his Allie cry and always tried to make a funny face to get her to smile again. She would always respond with a pout, and he'd say, "Your face is going to get stuck like that." And that would bring laughter to the both of them. She smiled through her tear-stained face and sat up. She took a deep breath and reached for the other envelope, wondering what could be inside.

Just then, the phone rang. Usually the only time her phone rang was when someone called from her job.

"Hello."

"Alex? You okay?" It was her manager.

"Yeah, Greg, I'm fine. What's up?" She was wondering why he was calling because she was due at work in a few hours.

"I just got in to get ready to open for the evening and discovered our power has been off since last night. The generator kicked in, I'm glad to say, so we don't have any spoiled food. But when I called Entergy, they were unable to say exactly when the power would be back on. Someone ran into a transformer down the street."

"Oh, did anyone get hurt in the accident?"

"I don't think so, but I've decided to just close up for the night. Mondays are usually slow anyway. None of the regulars knew you would be in, since it's not your regular day."

"Yeah, right. Like that would make a difference. But are you sure you don't need me to come in? The power may be on soon?" She needed to be at the bar tonight. She felt too damned lonely in this apartment.

"Nah, you're supposed to be celebrating." They had given her a little party Friday night at work, which had touched her dearly.

"All right, Greg, but if you need me, you'd better call."

"Okay, okay. I'll see you Wednesday unless you decide to take my advice and take some time off just to relax and enjoy not having anything to do. For the life of me, I don't know how you put in the hours you do at the bar and go to school full time."

She didn't want to hear the lecture again, so she agreed to think about it.

"Goodbye, Greg."

He hung up and she just sat there at her table, wishing for something. Anything.

She picked up the envelope again, curious now as to its contents. She unfolded the legal-size sheet and a smaller folded-up sheet fell out. It was a note from Mr. Fontenot with two tickets stapled to it. She picked it up and read it.

> *Congratulations, Alexandra, on your*
> *graduation. Bon Voyage!*
> *Sincerely,*
> *Fontenot, Sherman, & Boudreaux*

It was two tickets for a Carnival Cruise to be taken at anytime. What would she need with *two* tickets? The only girlfriend she'd had no longer spoke to her. Candice Carwin, whom she called C.C., had gotten married during their sophomore year. Her husband, Devin Freedman, was a real jerk and had actually tried to hit on Alex at their one-year anniversary dinner party. After that, Candice had become distant and soon stopped returning Alex's calls, and when her Christmas card was returned stamped "no forwarding address," she knew she would probably never see her friend again.

Alex was heartbroken that her friend had moved and not said goodbye. She was sure it was because of the incident at the anniversary dinner. *Had*

Candice seen the exchange between Devin and me? Did she think there was something going on between us? Those were the thoughts that plagued Alex. She missed her friend and wondered where she was and if she were happy.

Alex put the tickets to the side and made a mental note to call Mr. Fontenot to thank his firm for the graduation gift. She picked up the other sheet of paper and realized it was some sort of bank statement. She had never banked there and wondered why Mr. Fontenot had given the statement to her. Maybe it was one of her father's banks. She thought they had taken care of all his financial business after he died. She had only been a freshman in college, but Mr. Fontenot had assured her that everything was taken care of.

All her father's debts had been paid and what was left had gone into an account to pay for her college tuition. It had seemed like a lot at the time, but her tuition at Loyola alone was over thirty grand a year, not including books and her rent. Mr. Fontenot gave her tuition checks every semester and gave her a spending allowance monthly for her living expenses. When she had become concerned after paying for the first semester of law school, Mr. Fontenot calmed her fears by letting her know her father had taken care of everything until she graduated from law school.

She had now graduated and assumed this was the statement to let her know what was left. She had been offered many jobs with several firms around the country, but had put off responding to any of them. I guess this was her reminder that her free ride had come and gone and she would have to start paying her own way from now on.

31

Alex looked over the statement and noticed it was in her name and not her father's. Her wide eyes scanned the paper.

Account opened by Carl J. Wyatt -June 7, 1999
That was only a few days after her high school graduation. The tears came again. Her father had opened this account for her only days after he found out he'd had an aggressive form of cancer and would probably only live for another six months. He had died exactly four months from the date on this document. She cried now, not for the loss, but for the love they shared. There could not have been another father and daughter that cared for each other as much as they did. Even now, he was still her hero.

Alex could in no way have been prepared for the next surprise that awaited her. The shock caused her to suck in enough air to survive three days underwater. She let out a scream that the hand over her mouth could not contain. Her heart beat wildly and she had to wipe the tears from her eyes to make sure she was reading the numbers correctly. Mind you, math was not her favorite subject, but she was pretty sure she had mastered place value. Her hands began to shake and the numbers blurred again, but she was sure she had read correctly. Ten million, three hundred forty-six thousand, two hundred eleven dollars and sixty-seven cents.

Her mind was whirling. She knew her father was successful, but this? Mr. Fontenot had always assured her that her financial state was not in jeopardy, but he had never indicated any figures to her at all. She'd grown up in a magnificent home in Baton Rouge, LA, but she had never thought of her family as being millionaires. Could this be correct? But just as she thought it, she knew in her heart that this was her father's way of making sure she would always be taken care of. Her father's words came back to her. "*My wish for you is to not have any financial burdens that may hinder you from following your heart.*"

She just kept repeating the unbelievable figure to herself, unable to speak above a whisper. To say the impact of it all was overwhelming would be an understatement. But in the midst of the shock was a twinge of excitement and relief starting to take shape. She hadn't felt anything close to this much excitement since her recent commencement. She was so moved at the ceremony and she knew her father would have been so proud of her, she just grabbed the first person she could. Professor Phoenix, unfortunately, was the unlucky recipient.

Alex didn't have a clue as to what she was going to do with all this money, but she felt like having a good time. It suddenly hit her that she had no one to share her joy with. Maybe she would go in to work anyway just to see if there was anything she could do. Just then, as luck would have it, the phone rang, and Alex knew Greg needed her after all. She was uncharacteristically giddy when she answered the phone.

"I knew you would be calling. The answer is yes. What time do you need me?" She was thrilled she had somewhere to go tonight.

"With this sort of intuition, you're going to make a brilliant lawyer. And seven o'clock will be perfect." The husky voice was traced with amusement.

Alex's throat nearly closed when she heard him. She knew who it was before she asked. Her voice, on the other hand, seemed to have taken a vacation. "Hello?" she finally squeaked.

"Hello," Joshua said as casually as he pleased.

"Umm, who is this?"

"Do you mean you agreed to go out with me before you even knew who you were talking to?"

"I thought you were someone else."

Joshua wondered if she were waiting on a call from a boyfriend perhaps. He didn't care. He was going to use her misjudgment to his advantage.

"Oh, that's okay, no harm done. Just give me the address and I'll be there at seven, like you agreed. Or would you rather meet me at the restaurant? It is a little hard to find, so it would be much easier if we rode together. Do you eat seafood?"

"Yes, no…I mean…"

"Yes, you want me to pick you up and no, you don't eat seafood, or yes, you eat seafood and no, you would rather drive yourself?"

"Hold on a minute here!" She couldn't understand why he always seemed to get her so tongue-tied. "First of all, how did you get my phone number, and second, I didn't agree to go anywhere with you."

"Your phone number was on the dry cleaning ticket for the jacket and you did agree to go out with me. When you answered the phone, you said you knew I would be calling and I did call. You said the answer is yes and I was going to ask if you would like to go to dinner with me on my last night in town. Then you kindly agreed to seven o'clock and I was going to ask what time would be good to pick you up. See, everything is as simple as that."

"I see." She couldn't help but smile to herself. He was right. It all sounded so simple when he said it, plus she really did want to get out of the house.

"My address is 5890 St. Charles Ave. and yes, I eat seafood. Do I need to dress up or is casual attire okay?"

He was waiting for her snappy retort and was a little taken aback by her almost friendly response.

"Hello?" she said, wondering if he were still there.

"Yes, I'm here. Casual is fine. I'll see you at seven…And Alex…"

"Yes?"

"I'm looking forward to seeing you again." She would never have admitted it, but she was looking forward to seeing him again too. "I'll see you at seven."

Then she was gone.

Joshua hung up the phone, wondering what had put Alex in such an agreeable mood. Whatever it was, he planned on keeping her there.

Chapter 4

Alex slumped down on her bed in frustration. She glanced around at the clothes tossed all over her room and wondered if women went through this every time they went out on a date. Technically, this was not her first date. Her dad had given Tyrone Phillips the third-degree when he picked her up for the Senior Sweetheart dance. She must be truly pathetic if in her twenty-six years, her dating history consisted of only Tyrone Phillips from a dance in high school. Would that even be considered a date? When her dad took one look at the souped-up Camaro he drove, he insisted on driving them to the restaurant and then to the dance himself. She was humiliated. No wonder no one even bothered to ask her to the prom. It was just as well; her father had been sick that night anyway. Alex smiled at the memory, then frowned again, because she still hadn't decided on what to wear.

"My goodness, how hard is it to find something casual to throw on? It's just dinner."

But just as she said it, she knew it wasn't just dinner. It was dinner with Joshua, an incredibly attractive man. And, oh boy, was she attracted to him. She had come to terms with the realization and decided there was no harm since he would be leaving in the morning. Tonight she would literally let her hair down and allow herself to have some fun for a change.

Alex decided on a pair of jeans and a red blouse that dropped at her shoulders. When she slipped on her sandals, the doorbell rang. She ignored her quickened heartbeat and cursed her trembling fingers.

She couldn't seem to get one of the tiny buckles fastened.

Joshua stood at the door, wondering if maybe he was a little bit early and had caught her still getting dressed. He could definitely offer his assistance. He rang the doorbell again. *Could she be trying to give me the brush-off?*

A knot formed in his stomach at the thought of not being able to see her again. *Get a grip man. She's pretty but she's not worth getting yourself all worked up about it. There will be plenty of women—*

"I'm so sorry, I couldn't get my sandal buckled," Alex said breathlessly as she opened the door.

Joshua just stood there, filling himself with her. How could he ever have described her as being pretty? She was a priceless work of art. He had never seen her with her hair down. No stretch of his imagination could have possibly prepared him for this. Seeing her dressed in her jeans and a blouse that showed off her golden shoulders, he could just imagine her long hair blowing in the ocean breeze. Even with the little heel on her shoes, her head only came to his chest. She might be petite but she was every bit woman. He couldn't recall ever dating someone her size before. Most of the women he dated had been quite tall. Here she was, small enough for him to lift with ease and to fit into all sorts of tight spaces. Without warning, images of her fitting perfectly between him and the steering wheel began to plague his mind.

Alex saw the darkening of Joshua's eyes and heat immediately rushed through her. She couldn't understand what was happening to her insides. He was standing there, staring at her wearing the hell out of a pair a jeans, and his scent was conjuring up some very stimulating dreams she'd had recently. His presence filled her apartment and made her feel a sense of safety she had not felt while living there. She knew instinctively she could trust this man and right away felt at ease with him being in her home. He would be the first person she had ever let into her private sanctuary.

"I'm sorry to leave you standing in the hallway. Please come in. I'll be ready as soon as I get this buckle fastened."

"Here let me help."

And before she could protest, he knelt to fasten her shoe. She looked down at him and had to fight the urge to let her fingers get lost in the softness of his curls.

She must have the smallest, cutest pair of feet he'd ever seen on a grown woman. She was just too good to be true.

"There you go. Shoe crisis averted. Are you ready?" Joshua asked, standing again this time, taking time to look around the apartment. It was small but inviting. The furniture and accessories gave off an Asian feel with soothing colors and simple designs.

"Yes, just let me grab my purse." Alex picked up the purse off of her desk and turned to Joshua, wishing she knew what to expect, but also excited that she didn't.

———

"Dinner was delicious, Joshua. I don't think I can eat another bite."

"Yeah, that will be *one* of the things I'm going to miss about this city."

Alex noticed how he stressed the word "one" but decided not to pry. She had to admit, after the pleasant time they shared, she thought maybe she would miss *him* a little when he left.

"Yes, I think I will miss the food too when I leave."

Joshua was surprised to hear her say she would be leaving. He had hoped he would see her again when he came back to take care of some business in the fall. "Oh, are you going to be moving soon?" he asked, trying to sound casual.

"Yes, I was only here to attend school. My home is in Baton Rouge, but I am still unsure of which firm I will choose to practice. I do know that though I have offers here, there is no future for me in New Orleans."

"I see," he said almost harshly. He was certain the "future" she spoke of involved her clawing desperately and alone up the corporate ladder.

Alex detected the change in Joshua's tone and wondered what that was all about. She decided to ask. "What is it that you think you see, exactly?"

"I understand that your future as a lawyer is important to you."

"Well, of course it is. It's what my father always wanted for me. It's what I've nearly killed myself trying to attain these past eight years."

He saw something flicker in her eyes when she mentioned her father, and he saw something else there. Uncertainty. The atmosphere was beginning to get a little strained so he decided to ask her about her father. "Is your father a lawyer?"

The pained look that clouded her face made him regret asking the question as soon as he had voiced it.

"Yes, he was," she said, staring at the napkin in her lap.

"Was?" he asked gently.

"Yes, he died during my freshman year of college."

For some reason, she kept on talking. "He was everything to me. My mom died when I was four so it was just me and Daddy."

Joshua unconsciously reached across the table and squeezed her hand.

"We were a team. Even with his busy schedule, he always made time for any of my school events and came to every single dance recital and all my tournaments. Whenever I could, I would go to the office with him and when I got older, even sat in the courtroom while he argued a case. Carl Wyatt was one hell of a lawyer and I always stood in awe of him."

Joshua had heard of him. Carl Wyatt had been responsible for some hefty fines being imposed on oil companies along the coast. Anyone causing harm to the Louisiana coastal wetlands would be ill-prepared, going up against him.

Alex knew the exact moment Joshua's hand touched hers. It gave her a sense of comfort she no longer thought existed.

"Your friends must have been a great source of comfort for you right after he died," he said.

"I never really had time to make any friends. I didn't meet my friend, Candice, until the following year and soon after, she moved away and we lost contact."

"Do you mean to tell me you went through losing your father all alone?"

"Well, there was Preston Fontenot, my father's attorney and good friend, who took care of everything for me."

"But who was there to take care of you?"

"I quickly learned to take care of myself. I'd been taking care of my father for several months during his illness, so taking care of me was not too difficult. On the other hand, taking care of my heart took much more time than I cared to give. Like they say, 'time heals all wounds'. It's been eight years, but sometimes I still miss him like crazy. This past weekend and today were especially hard."

She told him about the letter from her father, but omitted the part about the money.

Joshua wanted so badly to reach out and hold her. He couldn't help but admire her strength and determination. Just then, the waiter came and asked if they wanted any dessert. The bread pudding sounded heavenly, but she was so full, she was questioning the possibility of being able to get up from the chair.

"How about it, Alex, do you want some?"

"It sounds simply divine, but I couldn't possibly eat another bite right now. However if you don't have to get up too early we can get it to go and eat it later at my place. And you can even join me in a cup of coffee."

She hoped she didn't sound too brazen by suggesting he come back to her place, but she was having such a good time with him, she wasn't ready for it to end.

Joshua thought Alex was full of surprises. He didn't take her for the type who slept with a guy on a first date, so he was sure her offer was because she was genuinely enjoying herself. He also didn't miss the reference about joining her for a cup of coffee and decided to add one of his own.

"That sounds like a wonderful idea. I don't have to get up too early. It will be *my pleasure* to join you for a cup of coffee and dessert."

She smiled at him then and his heart nearly stopped.

"Alex, you nearly take my breath away when you smile like that. Do you have a license for it as well?"

The waiter cleared his throat, wondering if they'd forgotten he was standing there, but he had to admit the view was worth his wait. Alex's smile seemed to have him also transfixed to his spot. Joshua didn't like the waiter's attention to Alex one bit. He had no claim on her but, if only for this one evening, he thought of her as his own personal treasure.

"We'll have two bread puddings to go and we're ready for the check."

Joshua's hard glare directed at the man seemed to bring him out of his fog. Alex was totally oblivious to the entire exchange.

They spent most of the ride back to her apartment in comfortable silence.

"In response to your question you asked earlier; the answer is no."

His mental rolodex was spinning. He had no earthly idea what she was talking about. "And what question might that be," he finally asked.

"About my smile. No, I don't carry a license for it. It is nothing special and poses no threat to those around me."

"I beg to differ."

Joshua, you never have to beg me for anything. You should carry a license for being so insanely sexy. Just listening to his voice and watching his mouth move made her want to lean across the leather armrest and nibble his bottom lip.

"Alex?"

"Yes? Uhh… huh?"

"I said, I beg to differ." Did he detect nervousness?

"Why would you beg to differ?"

They'd reached her apartment building when she asked. He parked on the street in front of the building, then turned to look at her.

"Because your smile is like sunshine. Magnificently so. It's majestic, bold and commands attention. Your smile is bright, warm and the light you'd follow out of any depths of darkness. It's beautiful, Alexandra."

Darn it, he had done it again. Joshua had rendered her totally speechless. This was her night. The only night she would have with him. She unsnapped her seatbelt and leaned across the seat. She had to kiss him. She felt if she didn't do it now, she would die.

43

Joshua couldn't believe the timid little kiss Alex placed on his lips. Forces beyond anything he could control pulled her into his lap. He' known she would fit perfectly there. He quickly took over the kiss and explored her mouth thoroughly. She seemed a little unsure at first, but soon matched the fervency of the kiss. She gave back as much as he was giving. Alex was delirious with passion. She wasn't sure if this was proper date protocol, but at the moment she didn't care. She could stay in his arms kissing him forever. Forever?

Alex broke away from Joshua's mouth when she felt the bulge in his pants. She breathlessly moved back to her seat. How could she? He must think she was some sort of tramp.

"I'm sorr…" "I didn't mean to…"

They both spoke at the same time.

"You go," she said

"I didn't mean to take advantage of you"

"Are you kidding, I'm sorry. I practically threw myself in your lap." She averted her eyes and looked down at her hands.

"No harm, no foul, as they say. But to be totally honest with you, I don't regret it. I enjoyed kissing you."

She looked up at him then, "I enjoyed kissing you too."

They both were silent for a while. Both unsure what to say to the other.

"Well, do you want to come in so we can have our dessert?"

Joshua was enjoying the dessert he was having right here, but decided not to voice it. "Yes, it smells great."

As Alex and Joshua were entering the apartment, Richard, her next door neighbor, was leaving his. He stood there, stunned, with his mouth hanging open.

Joshua looked at her curiously when they walked in. "Old boyfriend?"

"He wishes. No, I am sure he is just surprised to see anyone come home with me. You're the first person I've ever had over."

He was confused. "Do you mean, you have never let any of your boyfriends visit you at your home?" He thought that couldn't be right since he was here and he'd only known her for a few days. "You've only known me for a few days and you let me over."

She put their dessert on the table and turned to him. "For some reason, I trust you. There's kindness in your eyes and a warmth about you that comforts me."

Her words touched Joshua. For some reason, he was glad she felt she could trust him, but he still didn't understand why she had not let anyone else into her home.

"So you are saying you never trusted any of your boyfriends?"

"No, I'm not saying that." Gosh, was she sounding like a total freak or what?

"Then what are you saying?"

"There were no boyfriends to invite over. Okay! Do you get it now?" She was starting to feel totally embarrassed with her inexperience.

45

"Do you mean to tell me, there have been no boyfriends since you've lived in this apartment? That's pretty hard to believe. I mean, look at you. You're gorgeous. You must have to beat guys off with a stick."

"There's never been time for anyone else in my life. I was too busy trying to become a lawyer." Alex was beginning to get angry. She didn't owe him any explanations.

"I see," he said bitterly, remembering similar words from Victoria.

"No, you don't see!" she shouted. "You don't see a young girl's life turning upside down and there's not a damn thing she can do about it. You don't see that same girl all alone in the world with no one to turn to. No one to quiet her fears, no one to make her feel safe at night, no one to laugh with, no one to cry with, and no one to make the pain in her heart go away! Do you see that, Joshua? Do you?"

She didn't realize how she'd gotten there, but she found herself engulfed in Joshua's strong arms.

Joshua sat down at the kitchen table, holding Alex. She had been strong for too long. He would be her strength tonight. With her crying softly on his chest, it took all the control he could muster to keep from carrying her to the nearest bed and making love to her until she forgot all the hurts in her life. She didn't need a lover now. Her heart was too fragile at the moment. She needed a friend.

Alex had never shared her grief with anyone and though she felt drained, she also felt lighter. Nestled here in his arms, she felt his strength lift some

46

of the burden of sorrow. She looked up at him then and gave him a faint smile. "I'm sorry, I lost it on you."

"I'm sorry I pushed you into it, but I'm also glad that I did. You needed to let go some of the anguish you've held inside for all this time. Though I didn't know the reason behind it then, I felt it even when you hugged me on the day you graduated. You can't keep things bottled up inside. It will start to eat away at you and soon you'll become an empty shell. If you ever need a friend to talk to, Alex, I'll never be too hard to reach."

"Thank you, Joshua, I may just take you up on that."

"I hope that you do," he said, and meant it.

They finally got around to eating the dessert. While they were, Joshua went into great detail about his new boat. He told her how he planned on spending his time, at least for now, traveling and living on it. They talked about their childhood, growing up. She told him about life in Baton Rouge and he spoke of his childhood in Boston. His parents, he confessed, were none too thrilled about his decision of traveling around on his boat like some pirate. Alex asked him what he thought about the different firms that were trying to recruit her and he gave his opinion, as best as he could. They were talking and laughing like old friends. It was exactly what she needed.

Joshua couldn't remember ever being in a comfortable setting like this with Victoria. All their dates had been stuffy social engagements. Not once had they really laughed and just enjoyed one another's company. As a matter of fact, he couldn't remember ever hearing his mother laugh either. Actually, Alex was nothing like any of the women he knew from home. Joshua couldn't understand why he was comparing Alex to Victoria or anyone else for that matter.

"I want to thank you, Joshua," she said after they both noted the time. "This was exactly what I needed. You've been absolutely wonderful."

"You're pretty wonderful yourself, Alexandra Wyatt." He knew it was nearly morning but still was not ready to leave her. "I had a great time tonight, and morning, since it's nearly five."

"I have a confession to make."

"Which is?"

"This was my very first date, not counting Tyrone Phillips and the Sweetheart Dance"

The warmth of his laughter made Alex realize she would really miss him.

"The very first, huh? Then I guess I am honored." It still surprised Joshua how sheltered her life had been. "So if you counted Tyrone Phillips and the Sweetheart Dance, how did I measure up?"

"There's simply no comparison; Tyrone bought me a corsage."

And with that, he laughed again and stood to leave.

Alex walked him to the door, missing him already. They had agreed to keep in touch and she promised him she would call if she needed a shoulder to cry on. His plane left at eleven-thirty and it was already after five. He would have just enough time to stop at Café Du Monde to have one last shot at their delicious beignets before heading to his hotel for a quick nap. When they reached the door, they found the same neighbor returning from a date. He had the same look on his face when he realized Joshua was just leaving Alex's apartment.

"Do you want to give your neighbor something to *really* talk about?"

"Yes…let's. It will drive him absolutely mad. I've blown him off for years. Joshua had intended on giving her a good smack on the lips, but when she reach up on tippy toes and wrapped her arms around his neck, that smack lost its way. What found her mouth was a full-throttle kiss that probably scorched the eyes of Richard, gawking at them. He realized she was struggling, trying to reach up to him, so with no effort at all, he picked her up and her legs instinctively wrapped around his waist. His hands unceremoniously cupped her firm, round bottom.

The best things did come in small packages, he thought. Everything she'd learned from their previous kiss, she explored, along with a few other twists and turns she threw in for good measure. Anyone passing by would have thought their kiss was the end of an all-night bout of lovemaking instead of two friends trying to trick a neighbor.

When breathing became necessary, he placed her on her feet and said, "I bet Tyrone Phillips couldn't top that."

"Well, I don't know, maybe I'll look him up and see."

Joshua laughed again. He had laughed more in the few days he'd known her than he had in a very long time. He cupped her face gently with his hand, "Take care of yourself, Alex."

49

"I always do," she said and gave him a smile meant only for him.

He clutched his heart and whispered, "If I ever get lost in a storm, I know that smile will guide me to you." He turned then and walked away.

Even though he was gone, Alex knew she would never be free of him.

Chapter 5

Joshua placed the last items in his suitcase and zipped it up. He wished he could zip up his thoughts about Alexandra Wyatt as easily, but he couldn't and wasn't sure if he really wanted to. Sleep had eluded him all morning. She was a complete anomaly. She was intelligent, bold, and had a strength about her that contradicted her years. He didn't know of any woman who could have endured what she had. And she had done it all alone.

But on the other hand, she was naïve, fragile, and inexperienced in the simple pleasures of life. Her father taught her how to take care of herself, but she didn't know how to do that and include others in her life. Her entire adulthood consisted of going to school and working at the bar. He wondered if she were afraid to let anyone get close enough to break her heart. The one friend she'd made abandoned her, just like she probably felt her father had.

She *had* opened up to Joshua. She was twenty-six years old and he had been her first grownup date. She'd even kissed him. Was it her first kiss? He was sure that it was. He remembered how chaste the kiss in the car had been before he literally pulled her into his lap and devoured her. Dear God! He had practically groped her while he kissed her goodbye as well.

What if his actions caused her to withdraw from the world even more? Did she feel as if he were abandoning her too? He needed to call to apologize. As he reached for the phone, he remembered how she had initially leaned over to him in the car, and she did agree to kiss him goodbye to give the neighbor something to look at. And what a kiss it was. It may have started off timid, but by the time their lips parted, she had kissed him with more passion than she probably knew she had.

He placed the phone back on the receiver. She was most likely still asleep, anyway. Before he left her this morning, he made her promise to go out and experience life. He believed her when she agreed. They had also promised to keep in touch, so he wasn't exactly abandoning her. He would still be able to be a friend to her. A friend.

Joshua picked up his bag, looked around the room and walked out. He had just enough time to make it to the airport. He passed the flower shop near the lobby. When he saw the corsages, he smiled, thinking of her date with Tyrone Phillips and the Sweetheart Dance.

Alex walked into the kitchen, looked at the empty coffee cups and dessert containers still sitting there, and let out a long sigh. After Joshua left, she had showered and dressed for bed but sleep did not come. Visions of their kisses consumed her. She remembered distinctly how her body rejected any conscious thought from her mind and shamelessly wrapped her legs around his waist when he picked her up. She had behaved like some sort of hussy. She realized then that she had experienced more firsts in the past few days than she had in the previous eight years. She glanced at the clock. Ten-thirty. He would already be at the airport. How could she miss a man who hadn't even existed to her a few days before?

She washed the cups and put them away, opened the refrigerator, and stared in there a moment before she closed it. She had no appetite for breakfast. When the doorbell rang, Alex turned towards the living room. Who in the world could that be? It was probably FedEx, she thought. Offers from law firms had been coming in for the past month. She looked through the peephole, prepared to tell him to leave the package at the door. She couldn't believe it. She swung the door open.

"What are you doing here?...Is anything wrong?"

Joshua had rehearsed what he planned to say to her on the way over, but when she opened the door in a t-shirt that barely covered her bottom, he couldn't remember his own name. Her hair was still down like he liked it. It was a little disheveled, like she had tossed and turned, but she was gorgeous.

Alex couldn't understand why he was there and the shocked look on his face had her concerned. "Joshua! What's wrong? Are you okay?...Joshua! What's the matter with you?"

Joshua heard the concern in her voice and remembered they were standing in the hallway. He looked around then, not wanting the nosey neighbor to catch a glimpse of Alex wearing next to nothing. "Umm…I'm fine. Can we step inside for a moment?"

"Yes come in." When she closed the door, she looked at him with her eyebrows furrowed, waiting for an answer.

"I didn't wake you, did I?" he asked, trying to get his mind back on track.

She just stood there. She placed her hands on her hips, which made the shirt inch up a little higher. He'd better bring her state of dress to her attention before he tackled her to the floor.

"I just noticed you were still dressed for bed and hoped I hadn't awakened you."

Alex looked down then at the short t-shirt. She hoped he didn't think she always came to the door like that. "Excuse me." When she turned around to go grab a robe, the view of her backside caused Joshua to lean on the door for support. "I'm sorry, I thought you were the FedEx guy." She said when she returned.

Joshua raised an eyebrow.

She threw her hand up and shook her head. "I hadn't planned on opening the door. It's just when I saw you standing there, I was surprised to see you. You are supposed to be at the airport. What are you doing here Joshua?" For the life of her, she couldn't understand how he was standing here in her apartment when she had just been thinking of how much she would miss him.

"I wanted to bring you this."

She hadn't noticed the gift bag he was holding. She took it but was still puzzled. "But you are supposed to be leaving in a few minutes."

"Just open it."

She sat on the edge of the sofa, offered him a seat next to her, then let out a soft chuckle as she opened it. She pulled the corsage from the bag and her brown eyes held a question when she looked at him. "You came over here to bring me a corsage?"

"Well, I wasn't about to be outdone by Tyrone Phillips."

"But your flight?"

"Can be rescheduled."

"But I still don't understand."

"Alex, last night you promised me you would start to experience life."

She looked at him, not knowing where he was going with this.

"Since you've been an adult, you have deprived yourself of the simple pleasures."

She looked away from him.

"Alex." He gently turned her chin so she would look at him. "The past eight years, you've lived for your father. You've done your best to try to be the person he wanted you to be, but now it's time to start living for Alexandra. And not that I didn't think you wouldn't do it on your own, but just like I was there for your first grown-up date, I want to be there for some other firsts in your life. Will you let me do that for you, Alex? Will you let me introduce you to the simple pleasures?"

Alex was desperately trying to remember how to breathe. He was saying he wanted to spend time with her. She wasn't exactly sure what that meant or how long he would be there, but she knew that if it meant he would be there for a few more days or a few more hours, she would treasure the moments with him. He was looking at her like his life depended on the decision she would make. And maybe it did.

Alex looked away from the intensity of his gaze and fiddled with the box in her lap. She knew he was waiting for her answer but for the moment she couldn't trust herself to speak.

Joshua was taking her silence as a rejection of his request and was sure he had pushed her much too quickly. "Alex I—" She turned again to him and placed her fingers on his lips. "I'm sorry, Joshua…"

She paused and Joshua physically looked defeated.

Her voice was barely a whisper. "I'm sorry, but this is all so new to me. You are truly too good to be true." She placed her hands in her lap again and looked at them.

Joshua wanted to pull her into his lap and comfort her but was unsure of what she was thinking. He placed his hands over hers instead. She finally turned to him again. He saw the tears threatening to fall and his heart nearly broke.

"Joshua I would like nothing more than to experience new things with you."

He couldn't help it. He had to hold her. Joshua reached out and with no effort at all, he placed her in his lap as the corsage tumbled to the floor. She buried her head in his neck, drowning in his scent. Damn, if this man didn't smell good. She reached up and softly stroked his beard. That mere touch electrified all of Joshua's nerve endings. She had no idea the torture she was putting him through.

He desperately wanted to make love to her, but this was not the time. Joshua sat her up in his lap and she gave him a smile that severed any negative thoughts about his decision to come here. He wanted to get lost in those dimples on her face. Joshua knew kissing her would have him teetering on the brink of insanity, but it was a risk he was willing to take. He cupped her face, gently kissed each cheek where the dimples miraculously appeared and disappeared and when he touched her lips, he heard the small sigh escape them. He inwardly smiled at what a fast learner she was. Before he knew it she was taking over the kiss.

Alex couldn't seem to get enough of kissing him. She wanted to explore every crevice of his mouth. She nibbled on his lips and for the third time thought that this was so much better than chocolate. His kiss was devilishly decadent. She licked his bottom lip again and gave a moan of protest when they parted. He was on the brink of losing control.

"I just want to hold you for a while," he whispered as he sat back on the sofa. "Okay," she whispered back and snuggled into his neck again.

Chapter 6

Joshua glanced at his watch and couldn't believe they had slept for nearly three hours. He looked down at the angel sleeping in his arms and wondered how she had managed to wiggle her way into his heart. But he knew the day would come when she would move on to begin her career and he would leave the world behind and literally go wherever the wind decided to take him. But for now, she was here, curled against him, awaiting new discoveries she would share with him.

She looked so peaceful, he hated to wake her, but his arm was starting to go numb.

Alex felt the gentle kiss on her forehead and prayed she wasn't dreaming.

"Wake up, sweetheart. New adventures await you."

"Do I have to? I seem to be experiencing lots of new things right here in this apartment."

Joshua could think of a few that he would like to experience, but thought it best if they actually left the apartment. "The object is to actually get you *out* of the apartment."

"Oh, all right," she pouted. She rolled off his lap and stretched out on the sofa. Joshua stood, reaching up to bring the circulation back in his limbs. He looked down at Alex squirming about like a cat from a nap. He could just imagine how she would feel squirming beneath him.

"Joshua?"

"Yes?" he asked as he sat and placed her feet in his lap.

"What about your boat? You were so eager to finally be able to take it out. And you said your parents were expecting you this evening."

"I called my parents on the way over and told them there was some business I needed to take care of here and had to postpone leaving."

"Weren't they upset?"

"Well, my mother said I was spoiling a surprise she had for me but other than that, they actually were thrilled. They think I've had a change of heart and decided to stay on at the university…They love the fact that they can brag to their friends about their son, Dr. Phoenix, who's a professor at Loyola. Everything is about appearance to them. And to have a thirty-four year-old son drifting around on some sailboat does not fit into their precious standards. They're afraid their friends will think I'm some sort of spoiled, rich playboy."

Alex heard the annoyance in his voice and wondered if there was more to it. "You aren't, are you? I mean you don't see thirty-four year old men retired and living carefree too often."

Though she said it jokingly, he knew she was trying to ask him about his character.

"No, I'm not a spoiled, rich playboy. I don't make it a habit to involve myself in meaningless affairs. And as far as living carefree, I've seen too many of my friends trapped in suits and corporate jargon, never getting to really enjoy the fruits of their labors. Sure they may have nice cars and homes, but what good is it when you're working eighty-hour weeks and your family has to go on vacation without you? They miss seeing their kids grow up and their wives usually end up spending more time with their therapists than their husbands.

"I didn't want to live like that. Though my family is well off, my brother and I inherited a substantial amount of money from our uncle when he died. I invested well and built myself an impressive financial portfolio. Now I am free to enjoy the things most people never get to do, though they want to. And as for my boat, it isn't going anywhere. You told me I've opened a new door for you. What kind of person would I be if I just opened the door and forced you to go through it all alone?"

She looked at him and realized he was just trying to be a good friend. She decided she could live with that for now. They could be good friends… that kissed on occasion. Couldn't they?

"So what do you want to do today?" He needed to get out of here. That sofa was looking too inviting.

"Well, I guess the first thing I want to do is call my boss and tell him I need to take a few days off. How long will you be here anyway?"

If it were up to him, they both would leave together. He could just imagine her standing at the helm of his boat with her hair blowing in the breeze, giving the sunset a run for its money.

"Well I hadn't really thought about it. Let's just take it a day at a time. I've already let the hotel know I would be there at least another week."

So she had a week with him. She already felt like she'd known him all her life. How would she feel after an entire week?

Alex got up to change. "Feel free to turn on the television."

Joshua found the remote and turned it on. There was a special report about a fire not too far from the apartment building. It looked pretty bad. The reporter was speaking to the owner who said the entire building was destroyed.

"Hey, Alex, come look. Isn't that place near here?"

Alex walked into the room, buttoning her shirt. She looked at the news report and blanched. "Dear God," she said in a harsh whisper.

Joshua turned to her then and was startled by her expression. "Alex what's wrong!"

She sat on the edge of the sofa arm for support and stared at the television. "I guess there's no need to call my boss for time off."

"Why?" he asked, following her gaze to the T.V.

"That's the sports bar where I work, or rather worked."

Alex spent the next few hours trying to get Greg on the phone. When she'd finally spoken to him, he assured her everyone was fine. They had already locked up when the fire occurred. Apparently there was faulty wiring in one of the generators which started the blaze. The sprinkler system didn't go on because of the power outage, which didn't make any sense to Alex. Unfortunately, the insurance would probably not be enough to rebuild. She was out of a job. She didn't need the money, but she had loved working there. Now she really had no excuse not to respond to some to the law firms interested in her.

"Alex, I'm sorry," Joshua said, reaching for her hand as they drove up St. Charles Ave. He'd asked if she wanted to drive by what was left of the bar, but she didn't have the heart to.

"I'll be okay, Joshua, but thanks."

"But your job?"

She looked at his worried expression and was touched by his concern, but he failed to remember that she'd been on her own for quite some time. "I took the job on the advice of one of my counselors. She thought I needed to have an outlet away from school. I guess it's high time for me to decide on my real job anyway."

Joshua didn't want to hear her talk about the career she would soon start.

"I do, or did, love my job, but I'm more concerned for Greg. That bar was his life. He put all the money he owned in it. It brought in a lot of money, but it was open not yet two years. They have two kids and one on the way. I don't know what he'll do. And the funny part is that he was more worried about his employees than himself."

"Man, that's rough."

"And it's not fair. He's such a good man."

"Sometimes bad things happen to good people, Alex. You should know that better than anyone and there's not a damned thing we can do about it. I know it's a cliché, but we just have to live each day to the fullest. We never know what tomorrow may bring."

She looked out the window and wondered what her life would have been like if her father were still alive. She seemed to lack the passion her father had for the law. At one time, she remembered, she had wanted to be a teacher. She had imagined herself being adored by a room full of tiny faces filled with question after question. What had happened to that dream? But just as she thought about the question, she already knew the answer. From the time she was born, her father had pegged her to be an environmental lawyer, working side by side with him. She loved her father dearly and did her best not to let him down. But was she letting herself down in the process?

They drove through downtown towards the French Quarter. Because of construction they had to take a couple of detours, driving them past the United States Court of Appeals for the Fifth Circuit. The old John Minor Wisdom Court House had suffered minimal damage during the storm and still looked as sturdy as always. Alex remembered her father showing her around and introducing her to some of the country's best lawyers when she was only twelve. Even at the age of twelve, she was being groomed by her father to be the next rainmaker. Alex noticed there were still several people hurrying in and out though it was nearing evening.

"If you want, we can just grab an early dinner and call it a day." Joshua noticed how pensive she'd become and figured she was still upset about the fire.

She cocked her head to one side and gave him a pointed look "Are you trying to back out on our deal, Joshua Phoenix? Per our agreement you…"

Joshua waved a hand in his defense. "I'm not trying to back out of anything. I just thought…"

"Thought what?"

"Never mind what I thought." He wasn't about to try to win an argument with a future lawyer.

"That's what I thought," she said in victory. "So where are we going?"

"I thought…I mean, I'm taking you to the French Quarter. I can't believe you've never been. Everyone should go at least once. There's a lot more there than drinking and transvestites."

She hoped so. She had heard some of the people she worked with talk about all the massive crowds and partying on Bourbon St.

They parked the car next to the river walk and right across from Jackson Square. Joshua had made sure Alex had on comfortable walking shoes when they left her apartment. He figured they would most likely be doing a significant amount of walking. His plan was to take her on a carriage ride, but sometimes there were none available if it was crowded out. The parking lot was on a slight hill; there were steps leading to the street. Before they reached the steps they heard hip-hop music and cheering. They soon saw the cause of the ruckus. A group of college-aged African-American guys were dancing and doing acrobatic tricks. Alex wanted to hurry down for a better look. She grabbed Joshua's hand and nearly pulled him down towards the crowd. Joshua just held on, grinned and wondered if he were creating a monster.

The guys were flipping all around and dancing in sync. Alex clapped along and danced to the beat. Joshua was wound up, watching her get excited. The guys asked for volunteers from the audience and soon one came along and took Alex by the hand. She looked back and shrugged her shoulders at Joshua as she was pulled away. The guy who picked her out of the crowd told her to get on her knees and put her head down.

She looked at a row of other audience members doing the same thing. The music died down and one of the guys did a flip over all of the kneeling audience members. The crowd screeched and applauded.

Joshua saw the volunteers stand up and shake the hands of the jumper while the other members of the group went through the audience with a hat collecting money. He wondered what Alex was whispering to the guy and felt a twinge of jealousy. He began walking toward them when simultaneously Alex and the main jumper started to run, then did back flips across the courtyard.

Joshua stood there, rooted to his spot. Seeing Alex flip through the air like that had to be the most erotic thing he'd ever seen. She ran toward him, eyes dancing and hair strewn about, just as he dreamed she would look after he made love to her.

"Did you see me!"

He saw her mouth move but her words failed to make it to his ears.

"Aw, hell," he managed to utter. A force beyond his comprehension drove him to pick her up like he had in the doorway the night before and, just has they had before, her legs wrapped around his waist. He wanted this woman. Alex had seen the determination in his walk and the intense look in Joshua's eyes. She was exhilarated from the backflips and was in no position to ward off the likes of Joshua Phoenix, and didn't want to. As if it were the most natural thing to do, she kissed him in the midst of the crowd with a fervor previously unknown to her.

No one seemed to pay any attention to them. This was New Orleans, after all. Seeing two lovers kissing in the middle of a crowd was pretty tame, considering some of the spectacles that were known to appear at night and sometimes during the day.

When he released her and brought her back to her feet, he held the tip of her chin and tilted her head up to look at him. "I've created a monster. That was incredible, Alex. Where did that come from?"

"Thirteen years of gymnastics."

Joshua thought about thirteen years of bending, flipping, and splits. "Mercy."

She laughed, knowing exactly what he was thinking. Alex made a decision. She wanted this man. She needed Joshua Phoenix.

"Alexandra Wyatt, you are temptation on legs."

She was back on her own two feet but still tucked in his arms. "I couldn't possibly be temptation…" Joshua was opening his mouth to protest, but she pressed her fingers to his lips. "Temptation is something you want but can't have."

He politely picked her up, casually tossed her over his shoulder and ran back up the stairs to the parking lot.

Chapter 7

Whoever is responsible for the endless "One Way" and "No Left Turn" signs in this city needs to be burned at the stake, Joshua thought. His hotel was less than a mile away, but he had to drive about four miles out of his way just to get to it. He glanced at Alex. She was looking straight ahead and he looked for some sign of anything on her face. Was he reading something into the meaning of her words? Maybe she only meant he could have her as a friend, a buddy, a confidant. But she wasn't questioning where they were going, either. Almost there, he thought, one more street to cross. Never a break. Crossing Bourbon St was sometimes like parting the Red Sea.

"I hope the hotel parking lot isn't too crowded."

She looked at him then and said, "It shouldn't be. Besides this street, it doesn't look like there's much going on tonight."

He breathed a little easier. At least she didn't protest to going, but maybe she thought they were going for dinner or something. He couldn't just come right out and ask her if she were trying to tell him it was okay if he wanted to have sex with her. Even thinking it sounded crass. They made it to the parking garage at last.

"Umm, Alex?"

"Yes, Joshua?" She turned and placed her hand on his thigh, with the sort of intimacy only lovers use. He could feel her lithe hand tremble slightly, but her placement of it and her darkening expression answered his question. Joshua didn't want to waste another moment.

"Do you have your purse? I'm just going to have the valet take the car."

"Yes, I have it." She almost didn't recognize the small sound that came from her mouth. She was nervous, but she trusted Joshua and wanted to share this with him before they both left to start new lives. She wanted to live for today.

The elevator ride seemed to take hours. They both stood in the middle of the elevator, staring up at the numbers. He was on the sixth floor. The elevator ding brought them out of their own private thoughts and they stepped out onto the floor. Joshua's room was right across from the elevator. Before he put the key in the slot, he turned to Alex, wanting to be sure of her decision.

"Are you sure, Alex?"

"Yes, Joshua, I'm sure." She knew he was aware she was a virgin and was trying to give her an opportunity to change her mind.

"Alex, I just want you to know I won't take what we are about to do lightly. When I make love to you, it will be something special, because you are someone special. I will always cherish coming together with you."

"Thank you, Joshua, for saying that."

She smiled at him then. The light kiss he planned on placing on her lips turned into an outpouring of passion that confirmed everything he'd told her, and more. They heard the ding of the elevator and at the same time, the hotel door opened from the inside.

"Isn't this cozy?"

They both looked up and Alex was about to apologize, assuming they were in front of the wrong door, when her words were cut short.

"What's the matter, Joshua darling, aren't you glad to see me?"

"Victoria!" Joshua growled through gritted teeth.

Joshua knew this woman, she realized. They weren't in front of the wrong door. There was a woman in his room, wearing next to nothing.

Joshua turned to look at Alex and her expression nearly tore out his insides. "Alex..."

She turned and slid into the elevator before the doors closed.

Alex stared at the buttons, not knowing what to push or where to go. Her trembling fingers found the button to the lobby level. She just needed to get out of there. How could I be so stupid? All sorts of questions took over her ability to think coherently. Who was that woman? Why was she in Joshua's room? Was he married? She had not thought to ask. Was she just another conquest to him? How in the world did she let things get this far? The doors opened to the crowded lobby. She ran, ignoring the curious looks. If she could just get outside, she might be able to breathe again.

Joshua glared at Victoria and spoke through clenched teeth. "I don't know what broom you flew in on, but I suggest you get it and take it back to hell where you belong."

Joshua had to reach Alex. Knowing it might take a while for the elevator to return, he stormed through the stairwell. He could only imagine what she was thinking. He burst through the door at the lobby level and scanned the area for Alex. He saw her going out to a side street.

"Alex!"

She turned to him and continued to exit the building.

Damn it. Joshua nearly knocked over an elderly woman. After apologizing and making sure she was okay, he hurried after Alex. When he reached the door, he saw her drive away in a cab. "Damn it!" he roared as he threw his head back with his hands on his forehead.

"Whateva tis, she'll fo'give ya."

Joshua was bent over with his hands on his knees, trying to catch his breath, when he turned to look into the dark, wrinkled face of the elderly doorman.

"What makes you think so?"

"Tell by da tears. I seen lotsa tears in m'day. Know what kinda hurts folks have by da tears dey shed… Dem tears she had… well dey said she was unsho 'bout sometin'. Unsho bout you, I'm 'summin."

The old doorman probably assumed correctly. It was just as well. They would be parting ways soon anyway. But he just couldn't let her go away, thinking the worst of him. He was sure she wouldn't see him now and decided to go to her apartment first thing in the morning.

Victoria had the good sense to be gone by the time he entered his hotel room. On his way back up, he'd stopped by the front desk and requested to speak to the manager. He wanted to know who was responsible for letting Victoria Johnson into his room. He was willing to bet his new boat his mother had something to do with her sudden appearance. It had been several years since he had seen her last, but his brother mentioned recently she had moved back to Boston.

The hotel manager spoke to several desk clerks and one confessed Victoria had given a convincing story of being his fiancé and very much wanted to surprise him. She'd told them Dr. Phoenix recently extended his stay, waiting for her arrival from Europe. The manager apologized profusely and assured Joshua the clerk would be reprimanded, Joshua didn't want the young man to suffer any harm due to Victoria's wrongdoings and insisted there was no harm done. That, of course, was a lie, because Alex had run out on him. He wasn't too convinced he would be able to get her to listen to him.

Joshua was sitting in his car, still trying to think of something that would convince Alex he had nothing to do with Victoria being in his hotel room. His cell phone rang. Who in the world would be calling this early? It was 8:00am He had already gotten a few curious stares from a few people jogging by.

"Hello."

"I understand you had a visitor last night."

Joshua smiled for the first time since Alex left on that elevator. He recognized the voice of his brother immediately.

"Hey, big' bro, I see the friendly skies have let you go long enough for you to talk to Mom…How are you?"

Landon Phoenix was a pilot for British Airways and a devout bachelor. He was only a year and a half older than Joshua, but Joshua never let him forget it.

"Oh, I can't complain. Europe has been breathtaking this time of the year."

Joshua knew full well that his brother's breathtaking scenery had nothing to do with the landscape or the weather.

"You don't say."

"Really, Josh, you should meet me in New York for my next flight to Heathrow in a couple of weeks. I'll be there a few days, then I fly to Charles DeGaulle in Paris. Bro, the women in Paris love brothers."

"Naw, man, I'll pass. The ocean has been calling for far too long."

"Well, from the way things sound, there's something keeping you from it or shall I say someone?"

"It damn sure isn't Victoria Johnson, if that's what you're thinking. That ship sailed long ago and sank like the *Titanic*."

Landon couldn't help laughing at his brother. He wished he would have been there when Victoria showed up.

"Yeah, well you know Mom has always thought Victoria would come around and realize what a catch she let slip back in the pond. I don't know what you ever saw in her anyway. She was always a cold hearted bitch."

He heard Joshua groan and decided to ease up.

"Whatever, man, I'm just hoping she was great in bed."

Joshua rolled his eyes up to the ceiling of the car.

"Landon, was there a particular reason you called?" he asked, trying to get his brother to come to the point.

"I actually was just checking on you. I stopped in to see the folks last night and Mom was having a tizzy fit. She told me she sent Victoria to New Orleans to see you, hoping you would realize that 'though her priorities were misguided,' she's still a suitable match for you. She told me in so many words that you sent her away, not even giving the 'poor woman' a chance to talk. So, of course, knowing your feelings for the…shall I say…witch, I thought it best to call to make sure you didn't need any bail money and a good attorney for the murder charges."

"Well, fortunately, there was no murder, but she did leave a big mess and finding an attorney is the least of my problems."

Landon liked the sound of this. Could his little brother finally have met someone that piqued his interest? "Do tell, brother, and hurry; I have a flight in about fifteen minutes."

"Goodbye, Landon, have a safe flight." He didn't bother waiting for a reply.

Joshua rang the doorbell for the second time and waited. Maybe she was still asleep. They hadn't gotten much sleep in the past couple of days, or at least he hadn't. There were only four apartments in the building and his was the only one with a newspaper in front of the door. She had to still be in there. Bam! Bam! Bam!

"Alex! Open the door. I need to talk to you!" He nearly shook the building, pounding on the barrier keeping him from his woman. His Woman?

Richard stepped out on the walkway, giving him a smug look. As if he wanted to say, 'Oh, you're not kissing at the door *this* morning, are you?'

Joshua put his hands down to his sides and turned fully to face Richard, giving him a look that would have unnerved Hitler. Richard literally backed away and was about to step into his apartment when he turned to Joshua.

"You can knock the door down and she still wouldn't hear you."

"What are you talking about?" he said in such a way to make the other think twice about his response.

"Ease up, man. I saw her leaving last night about midnight. And she had a suitcase with her. Looked to me like she was going out of town."

"You being straight with me?"

Richard put his hands up in defense. "Look, I have no reason to lie to you. To each his own. Now me, I prefer a woman that has a little warmth to her."

Joshua wanted to smash this dude's face in for insinuating Alex was a cold woman, but Richard stepped inside and closed the door. Joshua turned and walk back to his car. It was a beautiful morning and there were joggers and moms pushing strollers all along the street, but he was oblivious to it all.

She left. And with a suitcase. Where could she have gone?

He could only think of one place. He didn't know why he had such a driving need to leave her with a good impression, but he was hellbent on finding her

74

so he could explain things. Joshua drove back to the hotel to check out, not knowing how long it would take to convince her she had meant more to him than a roll in the sack.

Chapter 8

Alex sat in the kitchen of her childhood home, looking at the picturesque scene through the French doors. She hadn't been there since evacuating from Hurricane Katrina. She'd stopped at the market on the way to the house, but everything was always clean and tidy awaiting her arrival, thanks to Carla Faye Briggs. Carla Faye had been a godsend to Carl Wyatt. She took care of all the housework when Alex was a small girl and transported her to and from gymnastic practice on the rare occasions her father wasn't available. Carla Faye was also an excellent cook, but Carl prepared dinner for himself and his daughter on most nights.

Alex could tell Carla Faye had recently made one of her twice-monthly visits to the house because she could still smell the lemony scent of the furniture polish. Carla Faye also made sure the service came to tend the yard. The two-story house sat on about five acres of beautifully manicured property. To anyone passing by, it looked as if there were a happy family living inside, bustling with activity. She didn't think she could ever consider the possibility of selling her father's house. This was the place she always felt safe and comforted. She had actually thought of the prospect of moving back to Baton Rouge until she figured out which firm she would choose, but she didn't want to keep her apartment belongings in storage until she found another place, wherever she ended up.

Cupping her favorite mug, she took a sip of orange juice and wondered if she closed her eyes and pretended hard enough, she could make it as if the last few days had never happened. If only she could open the pages of her life and just erase the chapter that included Joshua Phoenix. It was as if he'd materialized out of thin air and then was gone. If not for the blister she had received from her tumbling act, she would easily have thought she'd finally been disconnected from her faculties. After all the years of pushing herself to the edge and barely hanging on, she felt entitled to a breakdown.

She relished the thought of embracing insanity. Surely then she wouldn't be accountable for the ache accosting her emotions and the other awakenings exploding inside. The moment her eyes closed, he became more vivid. The mere touch of her hand on his leg had stirred up his manhood and in return sent a raging inferno coursing through her own body. My goodness, she didn't even know if it was normal to feel that way. Her body had come alive every place he looked, every place he touched, and the rumble of his voice created tingling sensations, causing her nipples to harden. The first time he'd pulled her into his lap, she was sure she would burst into a ball of fire.

Who *was* Joshua Phoenix? Was he a figment of her imagination? A hero she created to fill the void in her life? Why hadn't she reacted to any other man the way her body had reacted to Joshua? She'd had ample opportunity. Men constantly came on to her. She'd received flowers at work on several occasions from the more subtle ones and the more overt guys ordered drinks like Sex on the Beach and Flaming Orgasms. She had come across men who were absolute charmers and found it difficult to rationally turn them down for an evening out. But she had. Convincing herself she couldn't afford any distractions in her life.

Understanding why at this juncture she had allowed Joshua to sneak through her defenses consumed her. She had to interview with firms and would eventually be moving to another city, beginning her career; not to mention studying for the bar exam. This especially was not the time to get involved in a new relationship. Even as she thought it, she knew he actually hadn't offered her a relationship. He'd only promised to show her the simple pleasures in life.

Promise broken. The Pleasure Ship must have shipwrecked before reaching its final destination. All she felt was betrayed, abandoned, lonely, and horny as hell. Her body had only been introduced to the hint of something indulgent. She couldn't admit to herself that that was the crux of the problem.

She had dreamt once of a chivalrous man who shielded her from the rain. This morning when she awoke, could it have all been just a dream? A fantasy? Surely no mortal man rescued damsels in distress or took on the dashing appearance of a Greek mythical god. No mere man could cause intimate muscles to pulsate just by the sound of his voice. Yet she knew he had. She had been taken in by his flawless good looks and undeniable charm and was furious with herself for losing her resolve.

Alex didn't have an appetite for the toast she'd prepared and decided to adjourn to her father's office to make some decisions. Like her father, she chose to enter into the field of environmental law. There were several firms that were interested in her that dealt with the Louisiana coastal wetlands. They especially were in a critical state, and there was one prestigious law firm constantly involved in litigation with several oil companies that was interested in her. The office was here in Baton Rouge, but she was sure she would be in her father's shadow here in town. After a few hours of researching several firms, she narrowed down her list to two firms she wanted to interview with. One firm was in Boston and the other was in Los Angeles. They were a good distance away from Louisiana, but both were reputable.

Both firms were anxious to meet with Alex and had offered to fly her in for the interview. She sat back in her father's chair and rubbed her temples. The slight throbbing there indicated an approaching headache. She got up to get something to take for it and paused briefly to rub her finger along the spines of the law books. She turned to really look around the office. It looked exactly the same as it had the last time her father sat at his desk. She walked over to the beautiful standing globe in the corner that she loved so much, closed her eyes and gave it a spin. She stopped it with the tip of her finger and opened her eyes. This time, her finger stopped the globe on a place she'd not heard of in Niger, Africa, called Bilma.

She wondered what it was like there. She'd used to stand there often while her father worked, picking out places she would visit one day. She couldn't help but pull out her little pad she kept tucked between two books on the shelf, opened it, and wrote: Bilma, Niger. It was number 234 on the list of places she would travel to someday. She flipped the pages and looked at all the names of places stopping at Latvia. She loved the way that rolled off her tongue.

She would imagine herself calling the airlines and saying, "Yes, I would like a ticket to Latvia please." For some reason she would always say it with a Russian accent.

Alex closed the notebook and tucked it back on the shelf, feeling a little discontent. She had not been to one place on her list.   Of course she had traveled with her father in the States but had never left the country, though she kept an updated passport just in case. She continued her search for aspirin. The emptiness of the house was echoed in the padding of her feet on the hard wood floors. Once a warm, cozy place, the house now felt cold and bigger than life. Alex picked up the aspirin to check the expiration date and was startled by the sound of the doorbell.

It hadn't been too hard to find out where Alex's Baton Rouge home was located, but it had taken a little research on Joshua's part. Turned out Carl Wyatt's firm had given a fundraising auction for the Community Wetlands Preservation Committee at his home. There had been a huge write-up about it in the society pages. The firm managed to raise over three hundred thousand dollars for the committee. From the article he'd found on the internet, Joshua was able to locate the chairman of the committee who just so happened to be friends with the dean at Loyola University, Paul Bash, Joshua's good friend and mentor. In fact, Paul had been invited to the event but was unable to attend.

Joshua answered the call anxiously, "Hey, Paul, were you able to get the info I needed?"

"I still don't understand why you needed it. Wyatt has been dead for a while now." His southern dialect was laced with a Cajun flare.

"Yeah, I know, but did you get the address?" Joshua resisted a heavy sigh. Paul was deliberately toying with him.

Paul totally ignored the question and continued what he knew was probably torture for Joshua. "I seem to remember Wyatt having a daughter who was attending school here. Come to think about it, she was probably due to graduate this year… Hmm that's interesting."

"And what's so interesting about that?" Joshua said, squeezing the bridge of his nose.

"That you would be looking for the home of Carl Wyatt right after the graduation of his daughter. Is there a connection there?"

"I can neither confirm nor deny any connection."

"Oh…that's too bad…let's see here…where did I put that scrap of paper? You know I am so unorganized, I can't ever seem to put something down on this desk and find it again. I thi…"

"Okay, okay,…I give. Yes, I am looking for his daughter, Alexandra Wyatt. We are friends. She left town unexpectedly and I need to find her to clear up a misunderstanding."

Paul smiled, glad for his friend. He'd been after Josh to start seeing a nice girl since the ugly Victoria incident after college. And if he were willing to go through this much trouble to talk to her, she must be something special, no matter what Josh said.

81

"Well, dear boy, you are in luck; it was tucked in my shirt pocket all along. My friend at the preservation committee didn't have the exact address but gave me the name of the street. He said it's a huge house on a hill that stands out from all the rest on the street. You shouldn't be able to miss it."

Joshua hadn't been able to miss it. He had grown up in a large house but nothing like this sprawling piece of architecture. It was like something out of *Gone with the Wind*. The house exuded such a state of grandeur, he couldn't help but let out a low whistle as he drove up to it. He'd parked at the top of the circular driveway, wondered why he felt nervous and walked up to the door and rang the bell. As he stood at the door, he questioned if she were even at home. He didn't see a car but it could be in the garage, he thought. He was going to ring the bell again when he heard movement at the door.

What is he doing here? How did he know where to find me? Alex looked out the peephole again, furious he had followed her. She took a deep breath, pressed her hand over her heart and willed it to steady its beats.

Joshua was about to knock when the door jerked opened. There she was, standing there with one hand on her hip and the other on the door, wearing a pair of faded cutoff jeans and a college t-shirt. Her feet were bare, which gave him a brief opportunity to check out how adorable they were. He could easily see her swinging on an old tire swing in that outfit. He wanted to kiss that raised eyebrow right back into place and pull out the pins that held her hair hostage.

It occurred to Joshua, he had never seen Victoria not perfectly groomed, and painstakingly coordinated in her attire. Even when he'd spent the night with her, her sleeping outfit would be some sort of ensemble, and her hair never seemed to be out of place. All the years he had lived with his parents, he had never even seen his mother padding around the house in bare feet and an old robe. They both seemed rigid and cold, in a sharp comparison to Alex looking more beautiful than any woman had a right to be.

His appraisal of her did not fall upon welcoming features.

"You were not invited here and I would appreciate if you left." She had no intention of falling under his spell again and wanted him to leave her alone.

Joshua tried to sound casual. "We had an agreement."

Oh, he was trying that again, was he, she thought. There he stood, the mythical Joshua Phoenix, caped in self-assurance and storybook charm. Well, she had something to ward off his hypnotizing lure. She took one step back gave him a self-satisfied smile and slammed the door.

If Joshua would have been an inch and a half closer, he would have been looking for a doctor who specialized in rhinoplasty. He rubbed his nose, thankful it was still attached to his face. Well, that didn't go the way he planned, but if she thought that was the end of it, she was sadly mistaken.

Chapter 9

Alex pulled the drapes back slightly from her bedroom window. From its location she had a direct view of Joshua sitting on the front steps. How long did he plan on sitting out there? It had already been about two hours since he showed up. You had to give it to the guy, though, he was determined. She couldn't believe he was here in Baton Rouge. The poor guy had to have gone through a little bit of trouble trying to locate her so quickly. But it wasn't a question of how he did it, but why? He didn't owe her anything. She barely knew him, yet somehow she realized, he had become a part of her. She'd allowed herself to trust him implicitly.

Alex jerked the curtain back into place. "That 'poor guy'," she grumbled, "had a woman in the very room where he planned on taking me."

Literally taking her. The thought of making love to Joshua sent smoldering warmth to her most intimate areas. She let out a frustrated sigh, fell back on the bed and screamed into a pillow.

After a while, Alex sat on the edge of the bed and thought of the previous night again. Surely he had enough sense not to bring her to a room where another woman had access. Joshua appeared to be a bright enough man. But Mr. Stamps, her psychology instructor, had always said, "Common sense does not speak to everyone," so maybe he wasn't thinking at the time. Who was that woman anyway? The same questions kept surfacing, and only one person could give her the answers she wanted.

It was a warm day with a slight breeze giving ease from the thick humidity of the afternoon. The porch wrapped around the entire house on the first floor. The second floor provided a large balcony spreading the width of the house. If Joshua hadn't shown up, she would probably be sitting on the swing, relishing this break from the sultry heat. But he was here, and she knew she needed to deal with him, because he didn't seem to be going away.

Joshua had his back to the door as Alex stood there looking at him for a few moments. He was what fantasies were made of. He was the man who rode up on a white horse and rescued the princess. Joshua Phoenix was dripping with masculinity, strength, charm, and what surprised her most, warmth. He seemed to fit perfectly on her porch, sitting there in a pullover shirt and jeans. The contours of his back were apparent, even with his shirt on. He was a visionary work of art, she thought. And that hair. Why hadn't she taken the opportunity to let her fingers get tangled in the short, pliable curls when he'd lifted her off the floor and transported her to passions she'd not known before?

"Are you married?" Alex asked in a steady voice. She had to know. She had long since lost the battle of being angry with him and now was just annoyed with herself.

Joshua was about to stand at the sound of her voice, but couldn't. She had taken her hair out of the severe bun and had it pulled back in a playful ponytail. The ends were loose, giving her the appearance of a young girl, but her body was all woman. He badly wanted to pull her down in his lap and kiss the sweet innocence away down to the depths of the passionate tigress he knew was underneath. Instead, he just sat there, looking up at her. Nor did he want to seem overly animated that she had come out to talk to him.

"No, I am not married and never have been."

He saw her physically relax. Well, at least he knew she was not one to go for a married man.

Joshua reached for her hand. She hesitated only a moment and let him help her down to sit on the step next to him. She turned, braced herself with one hand so she could look directly at him.

"Since you don't plan to leave until you talk to me...talk."

She had an air of calm and self confidence which he found he liked a lot. Joshua was glad she was giving him the chance to explain, but was equally pleased to know she would not stand to be disrespected in any way. For the next forty-five minutes, he told her about his former relationship with Victoria and how she had come to be standing in the doorway of his hotel room.

Silence filled the evening air as they both sat lost in their own thoughts. Alex wished now she had not run out on him and had given him a chance to explain things, but she was touched by his insistence on not letting them part with such a misunderstanding. He was here at her home...again. Twice he had tracked her down. She looked at the car in the driveway and started to giggle. She had ridden in the car before but had not paid that much attention to it. It was a white Mustang.

Joshua looked at Alex and wondered what was wrong with her. She was sitting there giggling like someone was tickling her feet. He had not spoken of Victoria since she had chosen her career over him. He couldn't imagine Alexandra Wyatt turning into a cold, calloused, power-hungry bitch, but success and ambition can have a powerful lure.

"What's wrong with you?" he asked, smiling at her.

"Huh?"

"What's so funny?"

"Oh, nothing. I guess I should ask you if you want to come in."

"I was hoping you would," he said with a bashful smile.

"Yeah, and why is that exactly?" she asked with a little more attitude than she wanted to display.

"I need to use the bathroom." He had done it to her again. She was immediately embarrassed. Why did she always manage to put her foot in her mouth when dealing with this man?

"Oh, sorry."

"No, I'm sorry, Alex... I'm sorry about everything. I wanted to introduce you to new things, but nothing like what you experienced last night. It nearly broke my heart when I saw the look on your face and the knowledge that it was there because of me, made it even worse."

He wished he could make it where she never had to feel any hurt again.

She reached up and gently placed her hand on his cheek, noticing how soft his beard felt. "Joshua you had no control over that. Victoria was the cause and I made things worse by my reaction to it. I should have known you wouldn't try to take advantage of me."

Her tiny hand on his face was stroking a fire nowhere near the spot she was touching. And if he didn't move away soon, she would be taking back her last statement.

"Alex, your actions were justified. Though it doesn't feel like it, we've only known each other for a few days."

She was about to say something else when she remembered he had to go to the bathroom. They both stood and went inside.

"Alex, your home is simply beautiful. Why on earth didn't you stay here to attend school?" he asked when he returned from the bathroom. Baton Rouge had the most popular school in the state.

"My father was convinced Loyola had the best program for Environmental Law." Alex stood there, watching him walk toward her, not finding it odd at all that he was in her father's house.

"Yes, it is one of the best."

"Would you like something to drink? All I have is water, orange juice and milk." She knew he must've been thirsty from sitting outside all that time.

"I'll take some water, please."

She gave him a bottle of water and led him out to the patio from the kitchen. There were two rockers and they each took a seat.

"This is like something out of a storybook," he said after taking a huge gulp of water.

Alex tinted a shade, knowing she was the cause of his sudden need to quench his thirst. Then she thought about what he'd said. She thought it was right out of a storybook as well, but knew they were thinking of two totally different stories.

Joshua looked out over the property. It was simply gorgeous and he knew why Alex hadn't given it up after the death of her father. Surely there were several offers for such a tranquil place.

"Yes, I've always loved living here. During undergrad school I came a little more frequently, but now my visits are rare. When my mom and dad were first married, she told him she wanted a house big enough to hold lots of children and, when they grew up, their families as well. My dad had this house built for her and let her choose every single detail of it…"

Alex paused for several moments, then continued. "Even those roses over there near the front of the house, she'd planted herself. And after all this time they continue to bloom every year. After she died I think my father couldn't move on and love again, because there was so much of her still in this house and a part of this land."

She loved sitting there with Joshua. He seemed to fit so easily into this setting. She wondered how long he planned on staying. "How long will you be in Baton Rouge?"

He had never really noticed her southern drawl before, but it was something about the way she'd pronounced 'Baton Rouge' that was like the sound of a beautiful songbird under the shade of a magnolia tree.

"It depends," he said, looking intently at her.

"On what?" she asked.

"When I left New Orleans I didn't think about how long I would be gone. I just checked out of my hotel room and made my way west. I figured I'd find out my plans when I got here."

"You checked out of your hotel room?"

"Yes, I didn't know how long it would take to find you and get you to listen to my side of the story."

"I see."

"So like I was saying, it depends on you."

"I'm actually leaving the day after tomorrow."

"Well then, that settles it. I will be in Baton Rouge till the day after tomorrow. I can follow you back to New Orleans."

"I won't be going back to New Orleans right away. I have a job interview in Los Angeles. I'll be there for a couple of days, then fly to another interview. When I go back to New Orleans, I'm hoping it will be to pack to move to my new home. It's time for me to join the real world."

So this was it. Joshua didn't speak for several minutes. He didn't want to talk about her leaving him and he didn't want to hear about her job interviews. He was even more determined to not ever let her forget the time they spent together.

"Well, in that case, I'd better find a hotel quickly so I can change to take you to dinner and maybe even a movie."

He saw the disappointment cloud her eyes for a moment. Was she unhappy he would be hanging around? "I'm sorry Alex, I can understand if you would rather not…"

"You could stay here with me if you want. There's no hotel nearby and it may be more convenient for you. Plus there's more than enough room."

Her voice was barely more than a whisper and Joshua couldn't believe he'd heard her correctly. "You want me to stay here? With you?"

"It was just a suggestion. I mean if…"

"I'd love to stay here with you Alex."

She turned to him and gave him the smile that he knew would keep him awake for many nights to come. "Would you like a tour of the property?"

"Lead the way."

Alex stood, reached her hand out to beckon Joshua to walk with her. Joshua knew he was in trouble the moment their hands met.

Chapter 10

"You know, you've ruined me for the Olympics," Joshua whispered.

They were seated in the center of the back row. The theater was designed for comfort with reclining rocking seats and lifting armrests so that a couple could snuggle during the movie. They had arrived early for the show they'd finally agreed on, deciding to have a late dinner right afterwards. The previews hadn't even started yet and they both were surprised there weren't more people in attendance for the newly-released action thriller. It was a weekday, but school was out for the summer so they were expecting it to be crowded anyway.

"Oh? And how did I do that?"

"The gymnastics was one of my favorite parts of the summer games and after seeing you hurtling through the air, I won't be able to watch it any more without thinking of you…and more specifically how you made me feel."

She raised a brow and pulled herself back so she could look at him fully. "And how *did* it make you feel exactly?"

He gently tugged her to him, looked around to make sure no one was listening, and leaned over to whisper in her ear. "It was the most…."

The lights were turned down and the previews blared through the theater. He gave her a look as if to say, 'you'd better be glad you can't hear me now'. They both settled back in their seats to watch the previews.

"I knew I should've brought my sweater," Alex said, rubbing her arms. Joshua lifted the arm rest and beckoned her to him and as if it were the most natural place for her to be, she snuggled right in. She was beginning to feel quite comfortable nestled there, a little too comfortable perhaps.

"Sir?...Excuse me, sir…" Joshua felt the tap on his shoulder and looked into the face of the teenager. "I'm sorry, sir, but you and your girl have to go. The movie is over."

Alex felt Joshua stir, sat up and looked around at the empty movie theater; save the cleaning crew, they were the only ones left.

They walked out like two insolent children being dismissed from the principal's office. The lines had grown at the ticket counter and the parking lot was now full. Joshua opened the door for Alex and silently walked around to the driver's side. When he got into the car, he just sat there, not sure what to say. Alex looked pensively at her hands, unable to come up with any clever retorts about the evening thus far, either.

She turned towards Joshua, trying to hold steady a look of rationality but was betrayed by the intense depths of her dimples. There was a look on his face that registered disbelief, then quickly turned into a gleam in his eyes that tugged at the corners of his mouth. Neither of them could hold it back any longer. Laughter erupted from them like a volatile volcano. They couldn't believe they'd missed the entire movie. Moments of sleep had been few and far between in the past few days and had finally caught up with them. Cuddled warmth had won out over the blaring action

93

resonating through the dark room. They couldn't even remember watching all of the previews.

The last thing Alex remembered was thinking how good it felt to be held by Joshua again. It had taken a full ten minutes for the laughter to die down which had awarded them some curious stares from people passing by the car. Every time they had gotten close to trying to speak, the laughter would bubble up again.

As they sat there trying to catch their breath, Joshua desperately wished he could break the spell Alexandra Wyatt had on him. Her laughter floated through the car as if taking him on a magic carpet ride. He knew he was getting a glimpse of a side of her undiscovered by anyone else and it was a privilege he refused to take lightly. The simple pleasure of laughing had become foreign to her, but here she was, unreserved, unashamed, and carefree. Throwing her head back and letting all her inhibitions run free, she was allowing herself to awaken from the life of solitude she had created.

He, on the other hand, was becoming vulnerable. Vulnerable to the refreshing innocence, the quiet strength that feeds a young girl's losses and disappointments and still soars her to the top. He was becoming increasingly vulnerable to the ease of comfort they shared. Joshua was also defenseless against the driving need that had prompted him to seek her out twice. It would have been much simpler if he would have just gotten on the plane and left for Boston, as planned, but from the moment he'd been the recipient of her smile at the campus coffee shop, he

94

was spellbound. He only hoped the spell would be broken when they parted ways in less than two days.

Not since her father was alive had she laughed so hard. She remembered when she was twelve and wanted to surprise him with one of her cupcakes she decorated just for him. She walked into his home office to place the cupcake in the center of his desk so he would see it, but had to sit it in his chair to clear a spot for it. She was trying to arrange the papers in a neat pile when she heard her father coming in with some important clients he was expecting. Alex was not to go into her father's office when he wasn't there, so she hurried through the adjoining door that led to her father's bedroom. She was in such a rush to make a break for it without being caught, that she completely forgot about the cupcake. Unfortunately, her dad had found the cupcake, but not before he'd sat on it.

After the hour-and-a-half meeting, Carl Wyatt painstakingly showed his clients to the door without revealing the *gift* from his daughter plastered on the back of his pants. Alex walked into the foyer towards her dad with tears ready to spill forth a river. She saw the remnants of the cupcake on her father's new suit and stood ready for the punishment due her, but instead of yelling at her, he'd apologized for ruining her gift to him. That was the kind of man Carl Wyatt was. He saw the good in everything and everyone. Afterwards, they both laughed at how he'd tried his best to maintain his composure after feeling the cake squish beneath him.

"I guess I'm failing miserably in showing you a good time." Joshua's husky voice broke into her thoughts and she looked up again into liquid brown eyes that still sparkled from amusement.

"Are you kidding me? This is the most fun I've had since high school and the best sleep I've had in years. I can't tell you the last time I've been so relaxed…" She smiled that special smile he thought only reserved for him, reached over and placed her hand on his arm. "Thank you, Joshua," she said in almost a whisper.

If she were some sort of test of his will, he was surely destined to fail. Joshua didn't know how much longer he could endure the combination of her delicate touch creating pulsations throughout his body and the magnificent curve that graced her lips. He was a passionate man, yes, but he'd never had the urge to unleash that passion in the most intimate sense outside the confines of privacy. When it came to Alex, his sexual drive bordered on madness. At this very moment he wanted to kiss her senseless and replace all the sad, difficult and dark moments that cast shadows across her heart with excitement, stimulation, and new possibilities.

"So, tell me more about Dr. Joshua Phoenix. How did you get so interested in sailboats?" Alex asked, looking at Joshua.

They were seated in a casual restaurant with a lively atmosphere. Old Motown favorites played over the speakers and she could see several people celebrating birthdays. It was the type of place you came to to hang out with friends and to let your hair down. There were semi-circular booths placed throughout the establishment, some small for cozier dining and larger ones to accommodate larger parties. Alex and Joshua were seated at one of the smaller ones.

"Well…there's not much to tell that you don't already know. I grew up in Boston with both my parents and my older brother, Landon. After high school I was determined to go away to college and talked my parents into letting me attend Howard University for undergrad. When my uncle on my father's side got sick, I moved back to Massachusetts to be closer to home."

Joshua paused for a moment, thinking of his Uncle Cortland.

"Were the two of you close?" Alex asked, prodding Joshua to continue.

Joshua smiled, looking nowhere in particular. "We were closer even than my father and I should've been." Joshua's tone was bitter when he spoke of his father and Alex didn't know what caused his mood to change so suddenly.

"And you attended Harvard when you moved back to Boston?"

"Yes…," he said, still thinking of the special bond he had with his uncle. He smiled at Alex then and gave her his full attention. "I met Paul Bash there while he was on sabbatical writing a book. I helped him do some of his research and in return he taught me how to become human again after Victoria. Paul's really a great man. I agreed to return to New Orleans with him when I got my doctorate, taught for seven years, and at the end of my tenure at Loyola, I met a saucy woman that nearly broke my ribs and cheated me out of a cup of coffee."

"Is that right?"

"Yep…so that's me in a nut shell," he said, sitting back.

"Who got you interested in boats?" she asked again.

"My Uncle Cortland used to race yachts and was actually one of the best. When Landon and I spent the summers with him, we spent days at a time sailing with him. Landon enjoyed the adventure of sailing, but I loved it all. I wanted to know about everything. I wasn't satisfied until I knew everything there was to know about sailing and the boat itself. On one particular voyage we got caught in a really bad storm. The swells were so deep it was as if the yacht were sucked beneath the ocean for several minutes before we were brought back to the surface. Water was crashing in all around us, and Uncle Cortland and I were scrambling to stay afloat. Landon hadn't come with us that time. Uncle Cortland slipped and hit his head on the outhaul."

When Alex looked confused, he explained that the outhaul was one of the poles the sails rested on. When he was sure she understood, he continued.

"He was knocked unconscious so I brought him below deck and tied him down to keep him from being tossed about. By morning the storm had moved on, leaving blue skies and calmer seas. When Uncle Cortland woke and saw I'd singlehandedly kept us from drowning, he knew I was a born sailor. That next summer he bought me my own small sailboat and I guess you can say, that was all she wrote."

Alex was really impressed with the skill Joshua seemed to have and wondered what it would be like to be alone in the middle of the ocean with Joshua Phoenix. "When will you fly out to your new sailboat and what will you do with your car?"

Joshua wished Alex would be there when he saw the completed project for the first time. He didn't want to think about leaving her, but since she'd asked, he'd might as well face the inevitable.

"The car is a rental I've had for a while. I drove my car to Boston a few months ago to finalize some paperwork for *The Phoenix*. I will fly out the day after tomorrow."

They both looked up when Brian, their waiter, appeared with the food. "Ribeye for the lady and grilled salmon for the gentleman. Is there anything else I can get for you right now?"

"No, thank you,'" they both said.

"That steak is nearly as big as you are."

Alex cocked her head to the side and looked pointedly at him as if to say, "Don't let the size fool you".

Joshua raised his hands in surrender. "Okay…okay…I'm not going there."

They continued to enjoy themselves and the meal. Alex felt a little daring tonight and wanted to try something new. "I think I'll try one of those simple pleasures you keep going on about."

"Oh, yeah, and what's that?" he said with a smile and a little curiosity.

Alex didn't answer him but got the attention of the waiter. "Yes, ma'am, what can I do for you?"

"Brian, I would like to have a Screaming Multiple Orgasm on the Beach."

Joshua nearly bit his tongue.

99

"Sir, are you okay?"

Joshua couldn't answer him if his life depended on it. He watched Brian utter something to Alex, then walk away. He reached for his iced tea to help him bring his voice back around and nearly choked on it.

Alex didn't know what to make of Joshua's reaction, then thought about the drink she'd just ordered and thought maybe she understood. He apparently had never heard of the tropical drink. Alex leaned over and patted Joshua on the back, trying to suppress her laughter, but she was sure her dimples were giving her away. "Joshua, are you okay?"

"What the hell is going on here? Am I in the *Twilight Zone* or something? And what seems to be so funny?"

She could tell he was actually getting a little teed off.

"Calm down, you look like you are about to have a stroke. I was just ordering a drink." She had to stop the laughter now because Joshua actually looked like he was going through some things.

"A drink? I've never in my life heard of a drink called…"

Just then, Brian brought the tall, tropical-looking drink and placed it in front of Alex.

"Thanks, Brian, this looks great."

When Brian walked away, Alex looked over at Joshua with a teasing smile on her face. "I'm sorry, Joshua. I didn't know ordering this drink would nearly kill you. I've made it so many times and heard the name so much till it doesn't sound nearly as shocking I guess as it sounded to you."

"You said you wanted to try something new, then you asked that guy for a screaming multiple orgasm. I didn't know what to think." He wiped the beads of sweat that were forming on his forehead.

"And you thought what, Joshua? That I'd become detached from my senses?"

"For a moment, I couldn't even breathe, let alone think." They both laughed then. He had to admit she'd really pulled one over on him, but didn't intend for her to get the last laugh.

She told him how she'd made drinks for the past two years but had never had one herself and thought she'd try one of the most scandalous-sounding ones many of the ladies ordered. She took a sip.

"How is it?" he asked in a low voice that made her look up at him. Something about the way he was looking at her made her middle quiver.

"Mmm, it's simply delicious," she said, licking her lips with her eyes closed.

Joshua's body immediately responded to that gesture.

"You want to try it?" she asked, sliding it over to him. He took a sip and with the same intensity in his eyes he said, "Not even close."

She was puzzled. "Not even close to what?" she asked, sliding the drink back to her and taking another sip. Before he could answer, she rolled her eyes and teased him, "You hadn't even heard of the drink before a few minutes ago. Do you think you can do better?"

"Most definitely."

"We can just see about that when we get back to the house. The bar is always stocked, but we'll have to pick up a few things from the store."

"Okay, if that's what you want."

"Yes, that's what I want, 'Mr. thinks-he-knows-it-all'".

The drink tasted so good, she'd already drunk half of it.

"You'd better take it easy. Those tropical drinks have a way of sneaking up on you," Joshua told her.

"Don't worry about me, Joshua. You'd just better be ready to show me your skills in the kitchen when we get back to the house."

"The kitchen is as good a place as any."

Chapter 11

From the moment Joshua laid eyes on Alexandra Wyatt at the campus coffee shop, he'd envisioned her lying on a bed, her hair sprawled out like an angelic halo hovering over her head, with him ever so gently freeing her from her clothing. He'd pictured her that way on several occasions in the past few days, and here she was, this tiny figure engulfed in her massive mahogany four poster bed inside a room that would have made even Scarlett herself envious. And here he was, ever so gently removing her clothing. Not once though, in any of his mental pictures, was she passed out cold.

After Alex had finished her drink, she had insisted on trying a margarita, saying it was one of the most requested tropical drinks she made. Joshua warned her she was making a mistake. He told her she wouldn't feel the effects of the drinks immediately, but later she would. And since she was a first time drinker, one was plenty. He'd also cautioned her about mixing different types of liquors. Joshua couldn't believe he had to tell a bartender any of these things or that she had never taken a drink before.

She, of course, didn't listen to him, saying, "Weren't you the one to tell me I needed to loosen up and start enjoying myself?"

Joshua just rubbed his face in frustration, knowing she would have to learn the hard way.

The margarita went as quickly as the first drink, and by then she was starting to ramble and giggle a little more than necessary. She had only two drinks, but these weren't just any kind of drinks; they were Southern Louisiana drinks and here they liked their food spicy and their drinks strong. Joshua felt it was time to go, before things got out of hand. He had no idea how a first time drinker would behave, but he soon found out.

While Brian was presenting the bill and waiting for Joshua to give him his credit card, Alex jumped up, insisting on going to tip the bartender. The bar was not in direct view of their table, so Joshua couldn't see her once she rounded the corner. Brian was taking a decade to bring back the slip for him to sign. He was about to leave the table anyway, when the waiter finally came back. Joshua scribbled his name on the slip and headed for the bar.

By the time he'd gotten there, he felt like he was watching a scene from *Cocktail*, the movie starring Tom Cruise. Alex and the bartender named James, he soon found out, were having a race making a martini. To anyone else, Alex just looked like a lively young lady who enjoyed having a good time, but Joshua could tell she was a little more than tipsy. He knew her tight bun and seemingly cool demeanor shielded her joie de vivre, as they would say in New Orleans. Her passion for life was evident. He just wished she knew it was there and relished the joy of it.

Alexandra and James were pulling out all the stops, flipping bottles and tossing ice. They played well off of each other. It was as if they had practiced the entire routine. Joshua wondered if all bartenders were privy to this show of enthusiasm and somehow knew this was a special talent acquired by those who loved their job. Seeing Alex this way made it difficult to imagine her imprisoned in a business suit every day, catering to all the stuffy traditions the courtroom exhibited.

James finished his drink slightly ahead of Alex, having the advantage of knowing where everything was kept, but the crowd that had quickly gathered around the bar obviously whistled and clapped for the new star on the scene. He had to admit, Alexandra Wyatt was a damn good bartender. He could easily see why her boss appreciated her. A beautiful, talented woman in a sports bar had to have been vital to his business.

Joshua didn't know what she'd said to James, but as he walked up he saw Alex and James shaking hands and overheard him inviting her to come in and shake things up with him anytime. Though he had no claim on her, he didn't appreciate this James guy inviting Alex anywhere.

She'd better not give him my smile either, Joshua thought, as if he had exclusive rights to be the recipient of Alex's smiles.

Alex tossed James a bottle of vodka for his next drink order, gave him a closed-mouth, apologetic grin that showed the traces of her dimples and said, "Thanks for the offer, James, but unfortunately, I have a date with my destiny."

Joshua knew Alex was speaking of her impending law career, but took this opportunity to make his appearance. "Hey, Sweetheart, are you ready?" He'd used the term of endearment for James' benefit, but felt good saying it just the same. Joshua was sure she didn't realize she'd done it, but she wrapped her arms around his waist, gave him *his*

105

smile, and said, "For just about anything, Mr. Phoenix."

"I'll keep that in mind," he whispered as he placed a kiss firmly on her lips. Joshua held her around her shoulders and floated out of the restaurant with the help of the cloud he was standing on. He could feel the heat on his back from the glare James was giving him and floated a little higher.

"Joshua." The sound of Alex's voice brought Joshua back to the task at hand. She had fallen asleep in the car on the way home and hadn't uttered a sound until now.

"It's okay, Alex, I'm here."

She stirred a little while he was searching for a nightgown. He couldn't find any bags and assumed she'd unpacked them. Opening the top drawer of her dresser, he found a pink, cotton nightshirt. He'd already taken off the little top she had on but kept her bra on, because he was only human and could only handle so much torture. After he slipped the night shirt over her head, he unsnapped her bra through the shirt and pulled it off through her sleeve and even that had his heart beating a little bit faster. She was tiny; undressing her and dressing her was fairly easy logistically. It wasn't so easy ignoring the fact he wanted her, especially after the orgasm drink.

She was lying on her back still and the night shirt reached about mid-thigh. He reached under it to free her from her pants, fumbled around with the button for a few seconds until he got it loose, as quickly and carefully as he could unzipped them, and began tugging them off of her. He could feel the beads of sweat popping out over his brow. This had to have been the hardest thing he'd ever had to do.

Joshua felt the smooth lace her panties were made from and fought the urge to peek under her shirt to see them. He felt that would be an unjust violation of her privacy so he just continued to remove her pants. She stretched a little and rolled over on her side, bringing her knees up a little, trapping his left hand. She must have felt it there and rolled onto her back again. Before he could finish undressing her, Alex reached for his right hand and placed it right at her center and rolled onto her side; again trapping his left hand.

Joshua surely felt the stroke that had eluded him earlier would seize his body at any moment.

"Joshua," she moaned.

Alex began moving trying to move his hand around, but he was holding it rigid. His eyes searched her face to see if she had awakened, but she still appeared to be asleep. *What in the world is she dreaming about? Dear Lord, give me strength to get through this night* he prayed. He didn't want to wake her but he was on his feet, bent over her, while getting her changed for bed. He was in an awkward position and needed to free his hands. Just as suddenly as she'd grabbed it, she released her grip, bringing both of her hands underneath the side of her head. Joshua managed to wiggle his hands free and finally slid her pants off. He tucked her under the covers and went in search of a cold shower.

Alex's dream of Joshua's fingers trailing over her entire body leaving traces of fire in its wake was interrupted by someone pounding on a set of drums. The noise was deafening and she was annoyed it was pulling her from her dream. She reached for a pillow and the movement made the drumming even louder. Somewhere in the distance she could smell freshly-brewed coffee and she needed some badly.

Easing one eye open at a time, she realized the noise was coming from her head and she remembered why. She also remembered Joshua telling her not to have the second drink. *Is this what people feel like after having two drinks?* She was about to close her eyes again when she spotted the bottle of aspirin she had never taken the day before and a glass of water sitting on her nightstand. There were two pills sitting on a napkin next to the water. Joshua must have found them in the bathroom downstairs. She took them to try to get the banging under control. Reaching over to put the glass of water back, she noticed she was wearing the night shirt Carla Faye had given her in the eleventh grade.

"How in the world…" she whispered. *Joshua*, she thought. He'd gotten her ready for bed. *Did he see me in my underwear?* She noticed she wasn't wearing her bra, but could tell she was still in her panties. The thought of Joshua touching her and dressing her sent a pool of warmth nestling between her legs. She was delightfully comforted by the fact he was here in her home and had taken the time to make sure she was comfortable for bed. Alex remembered the smell of coffee and went to get a cup.

Joshua was not in the kitchen and she wondered where he was. Deciding her head wasn't ready for much movement yet, she reached for the paper on the counter. Joshua was obviously awake, because he'd gone out to get a paper. She absently flipped through the paper, thinking she hadn't felt this relaxed, in spite of the headache, in a very long time. Joshua Phoenix was replacing her empty world with warmth, friendship, and something else she couldn't quite put her finger on. She was having an awakening of feelings that were unfamiliar to her and she knew Joshua was the cause of it all. Alex felt alive and looked forward to each new day.

Alexandra traced the words on the cup she was holding with her finger tip. *#1 DAD*. She'd given her father the cup for Father's Day. He didn't care that it was slightly misshapen. All that mattered was that it was a gift from his daughter, a gift she'd made with her own hands. During a semester on pottery in art class, she'd made the cup and painted it bright orange with brown letters. Carl Wyatt loved the mug and used it exclusively for his morning coffee. She sat there, looking at the mug, then looking around the kitchen, feeling the love she and her father had shared in it. She no longer felt sadness and loss; she felt happy. Truly happy.

Alex rubbed her temples and felt relieved that the headache was subsiding. She thought of the nightshirt she was wearing and felt a little embarrassed she couldn't remember anything after she'd gotten in the car at the restaurant. She remembered being behind the bar and the fun she'd had making the drink with James. She had to admit, being at the bar seemed a lot more fun than being in a stuffy courtroom. She thought about the sports bar and was saddened by the thought she would no longer work there or that Greg might not be able to afford to rebuild. A thought came to her, but before she could linger on it, something in the paper caught her eye.

Baton Rouge Gallery of Fine Arts
Presents:
Candice Freedman's
"Absence of Dreams" Collection

Could it be the same Candice she had gone to school with? She read the short biography of the new artist, but it gave nothing away as to her identity. Alexandra reread the article, but it mentioned nothing of a husband, though her friend Candice's married name was Freedman. She felt sure it was the same person. Candice's major was art. When she married Devin, one of the things she had regretted was quitting school and giving up her study of art. Devin wanted a wife to stay home and take care of the house and kids. The woman he married would not work and therefore did not need to pursue a college degree.

She had to find out if this could possibly be the friend she'd lost. She needed to know why her friend had abandoned her. Or did she think Alexandra had betrayed her? Alex had to find out. The first showing of the exhibit was later that evening and she planned on being there.

Chapter 12

"I know you told me you carried me to bed last night, but how exactly did I get into that nightshirt?"

Joshua wondered if Alex could read his mind because he just happened to have been thinking of her in that pink nightshirt of hers at that exact moment. They were on their way to some art exhibit Alex wanted to go to. She had mentioned to him she thought she knew the artist but wasn't sure. He still didn't understand, but had been pleased to join her on her shopping trip to find a dress to wear. She must have tried on about thirty dresses, but he had to admit the fashion show was nice.

She finally decided on an emerald green cocktail dress that had a hemline just below her knees and gave the appearance of classic sophistication in the front and an inch shy of being scandalous in the back. The back of the dress plunged down almost to her waist, revealing the most seductive back he'd ever laid eyes on. The color was breathtaking against her golden brown skin. He knew she would turn many heads in that dress, almost causing him to lie and say he didn't like it, but the dress was perfect for her and she knew it as well.

Alex had raised an eyebrow at Joshua when he picked out the perfect pair of strappy sandals for the dress. The heel was skinny and gave her another three inches. "What? You don't think I know what I like to see on a woman's feet?" he'd said in his defense.

For the evening she'd straightened her wavy locks, pulling her hair away from her face to fall straight down her back. Whoever's art was on exhibit tonight didn't have a shot once Alexandra Wyatt walked into the place. She was the epitome of elegant beauty tonight.

"I've already told you. You fell asleep in the car; I carried you upstairs, found you something to sleep in and dressed you for bed."

"Yes, I understand that part, but how *exactly* did I get out of my bra and into that nightshirt?"

He knew what she wanted to know and had a good time messing with her. "Look, I was just trying to make sure you were comfortable."

He didn't dare mention how she'd grabbed his hand or where she'd placed it. That was something he was sure she would be too embarrassed to recover from and remain comfortable around him. At least he wouldn't mention it yet.

She rolled her eyes, giving up on finding out if he had seen her naked and not really caring if he had. "Thanks, by the way, for the aspirins," she said quietly. "How did you know I would need them?"

"Life experience," he said, thinking of the time after Victoria dumped him. Alexandra saw the hardening of his jaw muscles and knew he must've been thinking of Victoria.

Alex told Joshua to turn and go up another couple of miles to the gallery. She had enjoyed shopping with him. She'd forgotten how much she loved it. At first Alex kept insisting that he go back to the house and she would get a cab home, because she knew most guys didn't enjoy the tedium of looking for the perfect dress. Not that this was some sort of special night or something, but in all actuality, every dressy occasion called for the *perfect* dress. And since it was her last night with Joshua, it was a special night for her.

Joshua had insisted he was enjoying himself, and whether he was or not, Alex enjoyed having him with her and getting his opinion on the items she chose. She'd teased him about how he would be the perfect husband for the wife of a shopper. He'd only smiled and said that was unlikely since he would be spending most of his time married to his boat. She'd felt mixed emotions about his statement. Alex wasn't sure if she wanted to picture Joshua with another woman, but she didn't want him to be all alone on his boat, sailing to the ends of the earth. He was too passionate for life, too much fun, and too damned handsome to be without someone to love.

Here he was, in the black sports coat and slacks she'd helped him pick out, looking like he'd just stepped off the cover of a fashion magazine. He didn't want to wear a tie so they picked out a nice cream-color crewneck shirt to wear under his sports coat. She just loved the contrast of the creamy shirt on his dark skin. This man was beautiful. *Who in their right mind would be able to look at framed art when this masterpiece is in their midst?*

No one seemed to notice Candice Freedman flip open her make-up compact with practiced ease for what was probably the tenth time in the past hour. And if they did, most likely it was suspected that the new artist was nervous or just wanted her make-up flawless for her debut. Candice wondered what was keeping her husband, Devin, so long at the office. It was just as

113

well, because ever since she had been approached with the idea of doing a show, any and everything would send him into a rage which, one hundred percent of the time, he would take out on her.

Tonight had been no different. She'd merely mentioned they needed to hurry so they wouldn't be late. She was expected a couple hours before show time. Before Candice could shield her face, he'd smacked her across it. "No one tells me when *my* wife should be anywhere." He'd spat the words at her like a man teetering on the edge of control. Candice knew the reason he hadn't finished the job he'd started was because his boss had orchestrated the whole affair of the exhibit and he had no choice but to allow her to show up. Bruises would let people in on his dirty little secret. In public, they were the perfect couple.

Devin dropped her off, saying he needed to finish up some work at the office and would return in time for the stupid art show. Finishing up work at the office, she was sure, was a lie. It was mostly likely he would be going to a bar, which he often did before he came home.

She had become so proficient at masking her bruises that not a soul ever suspected the hell she was living in. Not even her mother or father, who simply adored their son-in-law, suspected a thing.

Her mother. Just thinking of her always brought a smile to her face and warmth to her heart. Candice loved her mother just as anyone who had ever come in contact with Lillian Carwin did. Auntie Lillian, as she was known in the community, was purely a kiss from God. She saw good in everyone and staunchly believed that even the vilest human being would respond kindly to those who consistently displayed benevolence towards them. Some may take longer than others, but she believed eventually love and kindness won out over evil and hatred. She often volunteered her time at halfway houses to offer encouragement to those that had trouble readjusting to life outside of prison and also for those that were bitter because of the seemingly insurmountable obstacles they were faced with. She answered calls for the suicide hotline twice a week and had always managed to get the caller to see that there were other options to ending one's life. Auntie Lillian would do whatever was needed to help those in her community escape drugs, violence, and jail.

William and Lillian Carwin had married when they both were eighteen. They had been high school sweethearts and loved each other with an intensity that radiated around them. It took them seventeen years of marriage to finally be blessed with Candice, and they loved and doted on their only daughter, which only strengthened their love for each other. Even now, after forty-three years of marriage, their relationship was just as vibrant and loving as it was when they were first married. Candice had been so enamored with her parents' love for one another that she made a vow to them that when she got married, it would be for life. She would do everything in her power to maintain her marriage and stand behind the vows she would make to her husband and God.

So here she was, standing behind a façade of make-up, silently praying her mother's philosophy was true, that love will eventually win over evil, but she didn't think she would survive to find out. Candice showered her husband with the love and respect warranted him, but it never seemed to be enough. After they were married he wanted all her attention focused on him and the only times she was able to mingle with other people without him was when she was visiting her parents. Art was a forgone pleasure until his boss had noticed a painting on the wall she'd done and asked Devin about it. He'd given an offhand comment about it that suggested it was just something his wife had tried to do. As it turned out, Devin's boss was a huge art collector and was very interested in seeing more of her work. So because it benefited his career, she was allowed to paint again. But she had given up so much for him.

For him, she had given up college. For him, she had given up her job. For him, she had given up the only true friend she'd ever known. They were like the sister neither one of them had. For him, she'd given up Alexandra. She wondered how her friend was at times and had even mentioned to Devin once that she wanted to see her. It had only taken one time to mention it to know not to mention it again. No amount of make-up hid the bruises he'd given her. He'd made it sound like she thought he wasn't enough for her. That she was never satisfied. He tried to convince her that her friends would only be jealous of the lifestyle she had and would try to come between them. It had taken almost two weeks to recover from the beating he felt she rightly deserved, and she never mentioned Alexandra to him again.

Devin constantly belittled her talents and at one time had her thinking her paintings were worthless, just a school girl's ability to slap some paint on a canvass. But she knew better now. She knew she had talent or she wouldn't be standing here, getting ready to open the doors to a crowd standing beyond them. Some had come to see her visual triumphs through her constant nightmare, but many more had come to purchase what she knew in her heart to be only the start of something splendid. She knew something else too. She knew that tonight had been the last night Devin would put his hands on her and though she loved God and her parents, they would have to forgive her for breaking a promise to them. Tonight would be her new beginning. Her parents were on a cruise they'd scheduled before the arrangements for the show had been made, so they were not able to make it to the show.

She wished Alex could see her tonight. They had stayed up late many nights, talking about their dreams, and though Candice could not envision herself as being a famous artist, Alexandra sure could. Candice had been content with studying great artists and practicing their techniques, but Alex was sure things would be different.

As the doors of the gallery were being opened to start the show, Candice Carwin Freedman said a silent prayer for the friendship she once had and for herself. She also silently asked God to forgive her for what she knew she had to do about Devin. She had to leave him so that she could continue to survive, mentally and physically. And as if God were sending her a sign that she would be forgiven and everything would be all right, she saw Alexandra Wyatt walk into the gallery.

Chapter 13

"There's an element of sadness to this painting. Do you feel it?" Joshua asked, studying a small, unframed piece that was tucked in an alcove. The lighting near it was dim and the wall was stark white in comparison to the dark troubling colors used in the painting.

"How can I not? It almost breaks your heart to look at it, yet I can't seem to walk away from it."

"I wonder why there is no frame around it." Joshua commented.

"I think putting a beautiful frame around the heartbreaking sadness of this abstract would distract from the raw emotions that are meant to be felt while viewing it," Alexandra continued, studying the piece. "The artist was obviously experiencing pain and turmoil in her life when she did this. You can't fake or just make up the feelings that are exposed here."

"Wow, I'm impressed. Destined to be a great lawyer and cultured in the arts as well. That's a hell of a combination."

Alexandra Wyatt never ceased to surprise him. To most people, she probably seemed strictly professional, especially since she had been unrelenting in the pursuit of her law degree. He, however was learning there was a much softer side to Alex and wondered, though he knew she had the stamina for it, if she had the heart for the sometimes cold, cut-throat business world.

"I'm not sure how cultured I am. This artist just seems to know how to speak through her work. And as far as destiny is concerned, I'm learning it is fueled by the destination or determination of the heart."

Joshua didn't know what Alex meant when she spoke of destiny and decided not to press her about it. The show opening brought quite a crowd to the large gallery. Held in a section designated for new artists, the show was located near the front of the gallery adjacent to a private area specifically for entertaining. It also contained a series of walls; though not attached to the ceiling, they joined to form right angles throughout the exhibition area, making it difficult to see large groups of people at once. The ceilings were vaulted, displaying wooden beams and huge white balls for lighting, giving off a rustic but chic atmosphere.

Alex hadn't found out if the artist and her former roommate were one and the same, but she suspected they were. She used to tell Candice all the time how gifted she was, in that she had the ability to convey a message through her painting. During their sophomore year Candice had an assignment for art class to choose a word from a box, and then create a painting depicting the word. No one could know what word anyone in the class chose. When all the paintings were done and displayed, everyone had to guess what word was being represented. Candice's painting depicted two small girls, one slightly taller than the other, and two older girls. There was a passage of time hinted by shadows throughout, but it wasn't just the visual image that indicated sisters; anyone who looked at the painting could feel the bond the two girls shared.

Sisters. *Had their relationship not meant enough to Candice to speak with her about anything that might have been bothering her?*

"Alex?" Joshua couldn't help but notice how pensive she had become. He placed his hand at the small of her back and felt slightly cooled, bare flesh. Oh, and it felt so right. He couldn't begin to wrap his mind around the fact she would be leaving in the morning.

She looked up at him with the saddest eyes he'd ever seen. "Alex, what's wrong, baby?"

The tiniest of tears slipped past her lids and slowly slid down her face and with it, the wall that had been standing guard around Joshua's heart was reduced to rubble. He gathered her in his strong arms and prayed he could always shield her from ever being hurt again.

In the few days he'd known her, she had managed to slip in through the cracks of his defenses and plant herself right smack in the middle of his heart. He loved her. He'd told her the very first day he'd met her that he wanted that smile of hers always smiling back at him. His heart knew then what his brain had failed to see.

"What is it, Alex? What's wrong?"

He walked her over to an area that would offer them some privacy. She hadn't answered him yet, so he lifted her chin slightly so she would look at him. More tears spilled. He hadn't left her side so he knew no one could have said anything to offend her, not that she wouldn't be able to handle them if they did, but he couldn't figure out why she was sad all of a sudden.

"I'm sorry, Joshua…to fall apart on you like this."

"What is it, Alex? Let me help."

"I've just been thinking of the relationship Candice and I had, and it still hurts a lot how it ended." She was going to say more, but a painting caught her eye and she was drawn to it.

Joshua followed her, not really sure what he should do, but something about the painting was familiar. It was called "Sisters". Though it wasn't a portrait, he could clearly see Alex's likeness in the painting.

"Oh, Joshua, this was us. This was her tribute to our friendship. Candice did this when we were sophomores."

Candice Freedman had watched Alexandra from the moment she walked in the door. It had been years since she'd seen Alex, but she looked the same. A little more sophisticated and more beautiful, if that was even possible. She wondered if the man with her was her husband. Every look and touch spoke volumes between the two of them. Candice watched the man embrace Alex as if she were a precious jewel. They reminded her of her parents. Their love was obvious to everyone in their presence. It was something she wished she'd shared with Devin. Anything close to the sort of intimacy and warmth she saw being displayed by Alex and the man she was with, was only a long-ago memory of what she thought was true love. By the time she realized what kind of monster she'd fallen for, it was much too late. She'd made a promise she felt she was duty-bound to keep.

Candice watched Alexandra as she noticed the painting she'd done so long ago. She wondered what Alex was thinking, and if she should finally find the courage to approach her. All of her paintings had been in the gallery for nearly a week and had only been viewed by those that were in some way connected to the gallery or those who had sponsored the show, before tonight. None of the paintings was officially up for sale until the opening. She'd received a few offers already, but none of them compared to the offers she received for her portrayal of "Sisters". To those offers, she kindly said, "Not for sale." The curator insisted she show it because she felt it was an "emotional" piece that would show off her abilities. Candice didn't care how much was offered for it; she would not sell it.

Joshua was holding Alexandra again. She had told him earlier of the friendship she'd shared with Candice and how it ended. It was when they were eating dessert after their first date. *Had that only been a few days ago?* It felt like he'd known Alex for a lifetime. Just as he was about to suggest they leave, he felt Alex stiffen and tremble slightly. She stepped out of his embrace, stood tall and lifted her chin with determination.

Joshua looked back and noticed a tall woman with smooth, brown skin who reminded him of the actress, Angela Bassett, walking towards them. Her face, he noticed, was just as determined as Alexandra's but he saw the nervousness in her eyes that she was desperately trying to hide. He could tell she was a natural beauty, even with her heavily made-up face, and wondered why she would go through all the trouble of applying it. This, he thought, must be Candice.

"Alexandra."

"Candice."

"How have you been? It's been a long time." Candice's voice was polite and as steady as she could manage under the circumstances.

Is she serious? Does she really have the nerve to flaunt herself to me like we've been sending Christmas cards to each other over the years and just couldn't arrange our schedules to meet?

Alex wasn't sure how she should answer Candice. Joshua was looking back and forth at the women, unsure if he should step away to give them some privacy, or stay. He was about to do the former when Alex grabbed his hand and held it. He knew she was trying to tell him to stay for support. He could feel her hand tremble, though there was no outward evidence of it.

Candice looked down at Alex's hand as she reached for the man standing next to her. She looked up at him then and wondered if Alex were going to introduce him.

"Wondering."

Alex didn't seem to recognize her own voice and felt herself wavering at the courage she'd just found to speak. Joshua reassured her with a slight squeeze of her hand and she felt courage again, then something close to frenzy. Candice looked away from Joshua and back to Alex. She was momentarily confused by Alex's response and it showed on her face.

"You asked me how I've been. I've been *wondering*, Candice."

At first that was all that she intended to say before she let Candice respond to her, but whatever the emotion was that bordered on frenzy, it was beginning to take over.

"I've been wondering, sad, frustrated, betrayed, abandoned, and furious." Alex kept her voice low and steady, not giving in to the satisfaction of going off on Candice.

"Alex, I…"

Candice was cut short when a handsome man joined them and grabbed her at the elbow. It had been a while since Alex had last seen him. His hair had already started to recede slightly and there were hard lines in his face, giving the appearance of a much older man, but she immediately recognized Devin.

Still holding onto Candice's elbow, Devin shoved a hand out to Joshua.

"Devin Freedman. We hope you are enjoying yourselves tonight."

There was something about this man that didn't sit right with Joshua. It may have been how he was holding onto his wife like she was an insolent child or the way his eyes had lingered a little too long on Alex. Of course there had been many men admiring her tonight, but none had leered at her the way this man had.

Joshua released Alex's hand and shook Devin's. "I'm Joshua Phoenix and this is…" After releasing Devin's hand, instead of grabbing Alex's again, he put his arm securely around her waist and pulled her closer to him, leaving no doubt that she belonged to him.

"Oh, there is no introduction necessary… Alexandra, how have you been? It's been such a long time."

He reached for her hand, giving it what she called a prissy handshake. She quickly slipped it out of his grasp. That gesture further alerted Joshua's radar.

"Yes, it has been a long time," she responded coolly.

If Devin heard the coolness of her tone, he ignored it. "Excuse us," he said, turning to his wife. "Candice, dear, there are some people who wish to speak with you."

Candice knew there were no such people, but did not want to make a scene. She needed this opportunity to finally clear things up with Alexandra.

"Alex, if you don't mind, could you hang around a little longer? There are some things I would like to speak with you about." She knew her husband could hardly contain his anger by the way he had her elbow in a vise, but she didn't care anymore. She didn't care what he would do to her later; she had to make Alex understand what had happened. Her eyes pleaded with Alex not to give up on her.

"Yes, Candice, I can." Candice released the breath she didn't know she was holding and smiled with relief.

Devin Freedman, on the other hand, was not smiling.

Chapter 14

Daddy's little girl, all grown up. Damn, she's even more of a turn-on than she'd been when Candice first introduced us. Look at her coming in here with that sexy dress, flaunting herself in front of all these men. She knows she wants somebody to get all up under there and give her something only a real man can. Not like that fake brother with the curly hair. He can't give it to her like I can.

Devin Freedman hadn't taken his eyes off Alexandra since he'd spotted her talking to his wife. Alex and Phoenix had been joined at the hip ever since. Devin watched Joshua walk towards the bathroom, giving him time to speak *privately* with the sweet princess. He came up behind Alex who was shielded behind a wall and thoroughly engrossed in a painting. This was a real woman, he thought. Hot, willing and ready, unlike Candice, who couldn't find passion if someone drew her a map. He stood about the same height as Joshua, making him tower over Alex, just as Joshua did.

Devin reached beneath the layer of hair and let his hand slide gloriously down the length of Alexandra's bare back.

"Umm, that feels good…That was a quick trip," she said, still looking at the painting.

"Actually, it's been far too long."

The familiar voice laced with alcohol made her skin crawl. She immediately spun around and slapped Devin hard across the face.

"You little bitch! I see you're still a tease."

All the drinks Devin had consumed combined with the entire spectacle made over his wife's "art crap" apparently made him bold and irrational. He grabbed Alex and tried to kiss her, claiming she was playing hard to get. His hot, foul breath so close to her face made her stomach turn. She couldn't believe he had the audacity to put his hands on her. A swift knee to his groin and another slap across the face made Devin relinquish all decorum and pretense of being a nice guy.

He shoved Alex hard against the wall. The painting crashed to the floor, shattering the wooden frame. Still, the loud noise did not bring him back to his senses. He reached down, jerked Alex up by her arm and just as the blow from his other hand was readying itself to strike her, Devin heard a fierce growl a second before he felt himself being lifted from his spot and thrown to the floor. Joshua Phoenix's raw fury was the last thing he saw before everything went black.

Seeing that bastard about to hit Alex made fear and anger grip Joshua in such a way he could feel the blood quickening through his veins. He literally wanted to kill Freedman. And he might have, if he hadn't been dragged off him. He was sure Devin would at the very least suffer a broken nose and jaw.

The gallery was in pandemonium and Joshua's fist hurt like hell, but he couldn't think about that now. The men who were restraining Joshua didn't know if they should let him go or not. They relented quickly, noticing Alex on the floor, trying to sit up. Joshua violently shrugged the men off him while giving them a look daring them to stop him from going to his

127

woman. It was difficult for Joshua to get a grip on his emotions after witnessing someone intending to hurt the woman he loved. And he didn't dare think about what happened before he showed up or what might have happened if he hadn't.

"Sweetheart, are you okay?" Joshua asked, gently cupping her face.

"I was doing fine until this wall came out of nowhere. But before that, I did manage to knee that jerk in the balls and smack him twice."

She tried to smile, but Joshua didn't see anything funny about it. Joshua was mad as hell.

Candice had been unaware of the entire scene. She had needed to escape the pretense of being the perfect wife while Devin acted as if she were brilliant and the next best thing to her mother's homemade pudding. Devin had finally excused himself, so she had taken the opportunity to get some fresh air. The weather was still mild and comfortable compared to the upcoming stifling heat and humidity that would make the South its home until about October. The slight breeze gently caressing her skin seemed to reassure her mind about the decisions she'd made earlier that evening. Candice took a deep breath, said a silent prayer and turned to find Alexandra.

Candice heard the commotion towards the rear of the showing area. Wondering what was going on, she quickly walked towards a group of people gathered around one of the exhibit areas. Pushing through the crowd, she gasped loudly, seeing her husband sprawled out on the floor with his face covered in blood.

"Oh my god!....What happened here?"

She was wondering why no one was offering her husband assistance. People were just standing around, looking puzzled, and seemingly watching for her reaction. She looked around, feeling like she'd just interrupted a scene being shot for a movie.

Candice was beginning to feel a little dazed and overwhelmed when she spotted the man who had introduced himself as Joshua Phoenix hovering over Alexandra. From her angle of Alex, she couldn't tell what kind of condition she was in, but she summed up the situation quickly. Her hand immediately covered her mouth and tears sprang forth from her eyes. Ignoring her husband, she tried to go to Alex, but Joshua barred the way from anyone trying to get near her.

"I'm fine, Joshua. Help me up."

"No, just sit here a moment, Alex. What happened?"

She was trying to sound as calm as she could, for Joshua's sake, but was still a little shaken up from the whole ordeal. She was sure she hadn't sustained any physical injuries other than the bruises she knew she would have later from where Devin had grabbed her arm. She was having trouble believing what had taken place. She couldn't believe a man, let alone a married man, would act this way, and in public too. She remembered how he had stroked her back. She had actually been turned on by it, thinking it was Joshua, and the very thought of his vile hands touching her in such an intimate way made her feel dirty and sick to her stomach.

Alex began to tremble and the tears she had tried so hard to keep at bay burst through the dam. This had been such an emotional night for her, seeing Candice, and then this. It was all too much for her to bear. Joshua held her tight, wanting to go over to finish the job he'd started on Devin Freedman.

Devin was beginning to stir, which prompted a couple of men to check on him, though the looks on their faces showed they wished they could take a whack at Freedman, as well.

"What the hell happened?" he groaned, trying to sit up and finding it difficult to do so. Glancing around the room, he saw Joshua glaring at him through clenched teeth and vaguely remembered being thrown to the ground.

All this because Little Miss Goody Two Shoes thought she was too good for him. Devin looked up and saw his wife staring angrily at him.

"You see! This is exactly what I was talking about! I told you your friends would try to come between us! This little vixen tried to come on to me and when I refused her, she tried to make it seem like I was hitting on her when her man showed up!"

He was shouting as best as he could manage with his mouth all busted up. "Come here and help me up so I can call the police on this maniac! I think he broke my jaw."

He reached out his hand, but Candice just stood there, not believing this was actually her life. Her husband. It didn't go unnoticed to Devin that not only did his wife not offer him a hand, but no one else did either.

Devin Freedman narrowed his eyes at Candice and through gritted teeth he growled, "If you know what's good for you, you'd better get over here."

Because Joshua was trying to get Alex to calm down, he willed himself to quell the rage that was boiling inside of him, but Freedman's next statement sent him over the edge.

"You're going to believe that little bitch instead of your own husband?"

The man was obviously drunk, but not drunk enough to garner him any sympathy. Before Joshua could get to his feet, something inside of Candice snapped and her face became contorted with hatred, bitterness and fury. All the years of mental and physical abuse had taken its toll. She raced straight passed the borderline of madness and found herself drowning in it. Unable to see or breathe past the bruises, the constant ridicule, the loneliness, the pain and total hatred of the man her husband turned out to be, she let out a gut wrenching wail and descended on the man who had promised to love and cherish her until death.

The pointed tips and the seemingly inhuman force behind Candice's shoe surely broke a rib or two. It was all Devin could do to ball up in the fetal position and try to protect himself from the furious whirlwind pounding him. Shock, disbelief, and even deep satisfaction shone on the faces of those witnessing Devin getting the crap beat out of him by his wife. Though it wasn't talked about or even hinted at, many of those who knew the couple suspected he had been abusive to his wife.

They were too perfect. They never argued and she definitely never disagreed with him, not even in a playful manner. She never left her husband's side during office functions and she always seemed a bit uneasy around other men. Many of the wives in the office mentioned their suspicions to their husbands, but they refused to see it or stated it was none of their business.

Seeing Candice Freedman coming unglued made all those who had suspicions of any abuse feel uncomfortable, as if they were somehow responsible for the pain inflicted upon her. Not because they were concerned with the condition of Devin, but because many were afraid Candice would hurt herself, the same two men who had relieved him from Joshua, with great effort pulled Candice away.

Alex looked on the scene playing out in front of her like everyone else, in shock and disbelief, but something else dawned on her. Her friend had not abandoned her. Devin's control of his wife had kept her from her friends. Alex could not begin to imagine the hell Candice was living in, but one thing she knew for sure, Candice needed her. Candice needed to know she was still loved and though they'd been apart for several years, their bond was still strong.

Chapter 15

Alexandra insisted that Candice come home with her. After three hours of talking, crying and catching up, Candice finally drifted off to sleep. Alex sat up. She'd made up the sofa in her room so she could be near Candice if she needed her in the middle of the night. And since Alex herself had gone through quite an ordeal tonight, she wanted the comfort of being near her friend as well.

She sat there and thought how quickly life could change. One day she was all alone, and the next, Joshua had been there. One day she had a job, and the next day it was destroyed in a fire. Just yesterday she had no idea where Candice was, and now she was sound asleep in her very own bedroom. The evening started with her and Joshua all dressed up on a beautiful drive into downtown Baton Rouge and had ended with broken bones, an ambulance and a police report.

Alex pressed charges on Devin Freedman for assaulting her. He was taken to the hospital in police custody. Everyone was questioned and all agreed Joshua had acted in defense of Alexandra. Devin was also charged with domestic abuse. Alex had been shocked when Candice removed the top portion of her dress to have her bruises photographed at the police station. Her back was covered with marks varying from recent to a few weeks old. She didn't know how Candice had survived as long as she had.

Still in shock about what had transpired over the course of the evening, Candice was in no condition to be alone. She was glad to go back to the house with Alex and Joshua. For the first time since she'd been married, she finally felt safe. She'd also agreed to seek counseling for abused women. Not sure how her parents were going to react to everything, she *was* sure they would support her, no matter what.

Joshua sat at the kitchen table, fresh from the shower, wearing a pair of shorts and his robe. He admired the beauty of the table and the entire kitchen. The table was big and sturdy enough to last through generations with lots of children. He could easily see children that resembled him and Alex, running up to their mom, pulling on her leg, asking for a cookie. He tried to shake that mental picture as he continued to admire the kitchen. There was a large pantry and the cabinetry was simply a work of art. They were white with dark, solid wood counters. Everything had been crafted with such care and detail. Most of the cabinet doors were glass with wood frames. They were with individual panes of glass, like windows. There were two round columns that flanked the large entranceway to the kitchen, giving it the feel of grandeur, which is exactly what it was. He could easily see this kitchen being featured in any well known Southern magazine.

Joshua looked down at his bruised knuckles. The paramedics confirmed what he was already sure of. Devin Freedman had a broken nose and jaw, and thanks to his wife, two broken ribs along with several bruised ones. He also was thought to have suffered a slight concussion. He deserved much worse after what he had done to Alex and for what he'd done to his wife for years. No woman deserved to be any man's punching bag. He couldn't understand how a woman would stay with a man like that, but knew many did and often defended their husbands' abuse. He wondered if Candice would be one of those women, but after seeing her literally kick his ass, he doubted it.

He knew both Candice and Alexandra were probably asleep now. It would be a while before he could sleep, if at all. One part of him felt he needed to stand guard to make sure they were safe, even though Devin was in the hospital and in police custody, but the other part of him wondered what the morning would bring when it was time for Alex to leave.

Joshua had promised himself from the beginning that he would spend a few days with her and they would go their separate ways to start the next phase of their lives. He, however, didn't count on falling in love. He didn't want her to leave but knew he had no right to put her in the position of thinking she had to choose between him and her law career. And because of her faithfulness to her father, he wasn't so sure he would be on the positive end of the choice.

"I see you couldn't sleep, either," Alex said, joining Joshua at the table.

"No, I couldn't, but I'm hoping the chamomile tea will help." He gave her a faint smile.

"Thank you, Joshua," Alex said, noticing the bruises on his hands. She hadn't really had an opportunity to express her appreciation to him. "Thank you for being there. Thank you for everything."

"There's no other place I would rather be."

Alex felt that familiar stir in the pit of her stomach and felt her intimate muscles flex just from the intensity of Joshua's look. She wasn't sure how she should respond to the feelings she was having for

Joshua and decided she needed to busy herself doing something in the kitchen.

"I think I'd better try some tea, as well. I need at least a few hours of sleep before I have to leave for the airport."

There it was. The inevitable was spoken out loud. She would be leaving.

"Are you sure you're up to leaving, Alex?"

"I'm fine, Joshua. You don't have to worry about me."

"I know I don't have to, Alex, but I do. I would hate for anything to ever happen to you."

"Joshua, you can't follow me around all my life, waiting to rescue me." She sounded a little more irritated than she intended to.

Joshua stood up and walked over to where she was preparing her tea. He gently turned her around to him and hooked his finger under her chin. His voice was sensual and firm when he spoke.

"Alex, I don't think of you as some kind of charity case. I know you are strong and have learned to take care of yourself. You've suffered, you've been hurt, and you've done it all on your own. But the point is, you shouldn't have to. You should have someone at your side, loving you, shielding you from pain when possible, and when it's not, helping you through it. You're passionate, caring, brilliant, and a hell of a lot of fun."

Alex couldn't help smiling through the tears that were threatening to fall.

"You should be loved hard by a man smart enough to know what a special gift he has found in you."

"You think so, huh?" she whispered through her tears.

"I know so."

Joshua lifted Alex off her feet and sat her on the counter. He cupped her face and as if his life depended on her answer, he asked a promise of her. "Promise me, Alex, that if you ever need anything…*anything*, you won't hesitate to call."

At that moment, the way he was looking at her, she would have promised him anything. She wanted to kiss the smooth, dark brows that were furrowed in such seriousness. She wanted this man, Joshua Phoenix, not any other, to be the one who would love her hard and shield her from pains. Joshua Phoenix had been her special gift; a man who was determined to live a life alone on the sea.

The sun would bring forth a new day and new lives for both of them, but while the moon ruled the sky, he was here with her, and she, with him. He had promised her simple pleasures. She prayed the moon would keep the sun at bay while she spent these last moments taking pleasure in loving Dr. Joshua Phoenix. The only man that stirred her insides and the only man who would have complete ownership of her heart.

"Promise me, Alex," he said with urgency.

"I promise, Joshua."

It was barely more than a whisper, but he was satisfied. Before he released his hands from her face, she leaned towards him and began placing light, feathery kisses on his eyebrows, then slowly she began placing them all over his face. She hesitated only a moment when she glanced up at him before taking his moist, full lips hostage. They immediately parted for her and she wasted no time darting her tongue into the warm, familiar depths. She wasn't an experienced kisser, but she'd picked up a few things from Joshua in the past few days. What she lacked in experience, she made up with passion. And before the opportunity was taken away from her, she had to satisfy her urge to feel his curly locks. She reached up with both hands and her fingers gloried in the soft texture of them. This man was simply perfect.

So far, Joshua had managed to maintain control of his desires while Alex took charge of the passionate kiss she'd surprised him with. Her tiny fingers were sending him into a frenzy, but when she reached through the opening of his robe and brushed her hands across his bare chest, managing control was the last thing on his mind. He had to have her.

Alex felt the exact moment that their kiss went from passionate to downright erotic. She moaned shamelessly from the feelings he was creating. This man seemed to literally be generating a fire within her. Her feet were heating up and she had no idea what was going on between her thighs. It was like a dormant beast had awakened and desperately needed to be fed. There was a dull ache and the beast was pulsating out of control. She could tell her panties were drenched and hoped to God that was normal.

Alex couldn't keep her hands off Joshua. She needed the contact. She felt if she could just touch him all over, somehow he would always be there. Their kissing was dragging her to the brink of insanity. She needed more. Alex found the strength to tear her mouth away from Joshua's and with a voice streaked with desire she heard herself say, "Make love to me, Joshua."

Before the opportunity was lost to him again, he picked her up off the counter and carried her up to the guest room. Barring the house burning around them, he would love Alexandra Wyatt in every sense of the word tonight.

When he gently placed her on the bed and removed his robe and shorts, she had no fear. This was her knight in shining armor. This was the man who would always keep her safe. She had no fear of Joshua Phoenix. He was the man she loved.

"You're beautiful, Joshua."

That was not what he was expecting her to say. He thought when she saw what she was up against, she would run for the hills. He wasn't, by any stretch of the imagination, a small man and he knew she was a virgin. Alex showed no signs of nervousness. What he saw etched on her face was desire, trust and, if he didn't know any better, love.

"You're the beautiful one, sweetheart." He knelt next to the bed and when she started unbuttoning her silk pajama top, he gently moved her hand to the side.

"Please…let me."

His voice was like silk shimmering down the length of her body. *This,* he thought, *was how things were supposed to go last night.* And when he'd finally undressed her, he found she was perfect. Somehow, some way, Alexandra Wyatt would be his.

"Do you want a blanket?"

"I want you, Joshua. Only you."

139

Who was he not to give the lady what she wanted? He pulled a condom from his toiletry bag next to the bed. She watched him put it on and was glad he had the forethought to protect her. Again, he had thought of her safety. Joshua got into the bed next to her, deciding to pull the comforter over them both, just in case she was cold. She brazenly captured his mouth, trying to satisfy the fire that was building inside of her. She let her hands roam over him. He was well put together. He obviously worked out. It was evident in the ripples of muscles from his chest down to his navel. She felt totally at ease with him and had no qualms about exploring below the waistline.

Alex began to stroke his manly essence until Joshua couldn't stand it anymore. When she was finally underneath him, he had to wonder if maybe he was experiencing some sort of elaborate dream. He leaned down and kissed her everywhere, discovering in fact she was really here with him. She captured his head in her hands and looked directly in his eyes.

"Love me, Joshua."

With those three words, he entered her.

Chapter 16

Alexandra Wyatt glanced over at a sleeping Candice Freedman safely nestled in the plush confines of the first-class flight, flying thousands of miles away from the abusive husband she'd found the courage to leave. She could not imagine the kind of treatment Candice had endured to transform her from the quiet, caring, and loving person she'd known into the woman seething with pain and vehemence she'd witnessed the night before. Candice still had not contacted her parents, not wanting to bother them on their much-deserved vacation. She would tell them the moment they returned, hoping they would not hear it from other sources first.

Morning brought the near certainty Devin would be released from the hospital, if not already, and the strong possibility of his being released from police custody. With the already crowded jails, Devin's money and connections, it would be impossible to deny an otherwise respected man of the community bail for alleged domestic abuse. Though she hadn't come right out to say it, Alex knew Candice was terrified Devin would come after her. She had not only attacked him in public, she'd exposed his nasty little secrets, humiliated him in front of his colleagues and pressed criminal charges against him. The charges from Alex would be hard-fought without Candice. It would be his word against hers, since no one actually saw him molest her. But with the accusations from his wife and the gruesome bruises photographed by the police officers, this would account for Devin's violent nature, giving credibility to Alex's statement.

Candice had never stood up to Devin for anything before, and she was afraid that if she had to go home to face him, she would lose her will to take her life back. She'd been his puppet for years, and for years he had dictated her thoughts and actions. She'd given up control of her very being to him and wasn't so sure if she knew how to take it back, but knew she had to try. She was convinced he would eventually kill her or, despite the fact that she wouldn't have imagined such a thing before the previous night, she would kill him.

She had eagerly accepted Alex's invitation to accompany her to Los Angeles, though all she had was her purse and the clothing she had worn the night before. On the drive to the airport they stopped to buy Candice a travel outfit, a small piece of luggage and a few other things she would need before they would do some extensive shopping in California. Alex was grateful her friend had decided to fly to L.A. with her and not return to an abusive husband after a night of fear of the unknown and remorseful thinking, like so many others, she was sure, probably did. Alex knew Candice would have to harness the strength she'd found when she slammed her expensive shoe into Devin's gut and feed off it in the months and years to come.

"Can I get you anything?" The flight attendant's question broke into Alexandra's thoughts for the moment. Alex looked up at the handsome middle-aged man. He had striking grey eyes and his salt-and-pepper hair was probably the only feature that gave any hint of his age. She'd overheard him tell another attendant he'd just celebrated his fifty-first birthday. He was well-built with the stature and confidence of an ex-marine, without the gruffness, and Alex was sure he was often mistaken for a pilot instead of a flight attendant when hurrying through the airport. He'd been extremely kind to them and seemed to pay special attention to the comfort of Candice, as if he sensed she needed the extra care. Alex knew the man was just doing his job, but unless he had Joshua stuffed somewhere in that cart, there wasn't anything else she needed.

"No, thank you, we're fine," she answered and turned to look out the window. The view was an endless blanket of white clouds. She looked up at the movie but had no interest in it. Unable to escape the thoughts that held her mind hostage, Alex finally slipped into the darkness that lay behind her heavy eyelids and found herself saturated with images of Joshua Phoenix.

Just thinking of him assaulted all her senses. She could feel his sturdy, but gentle hands burning delectable paths of pleasure along the length of her, leaving insatiable pools of need at her center that only he could quench. She could taste the intoxicating effect of his kisses, sending her into shameless fits of lust. She could hear her name being torn from his throat as they both ascended into the pinnacle of ecstasy. She could smell the carnal musk as they both drowned in a flood of sensations so powerful that neither could move nor speak.

"Alex, are you okay?" Candice was awake, looking at Alex with concern etched on her face.

Alex opened her eyes and stared at her friend as if she were confused and out of place.

"Candice?"

"What is it, Alex? Are you all right?"

Alex had been so caught up in her thoughts of Joshua, for the briefest of moments she'd forgotten where she was and why Candice was there with her. She took a deep breath, looked around and felt her face heat up, as if everyone had been privy to her thoughts.

"Alex, are you feeling ill? You look flushed and a few minutes ago your breathing was a little erratic. Are you okay?" Candice pressed her for an answer.

"I'm fine, Candice; I must have dozed off for a moment." She lied, but she didn't feel like talking about Joshua. She wasn't sure if she would ever feel like talking about him. Candice reached over and gently took Alex's hand.

"Look here, Alexandra Wyatt. I've used the phrase 'I'm fine' so much until I've forgotten its actual meaning." Candice leaned in a little closer to Alex so she could speak softly, but she did not want Alex to take her words for granted. "We've been apart for a long time, but I know you are not fine…and it's okay… you don't have to be. We were sisters once and I hope we still can be."

Alex gave her a reassuring smile. "Of course, we can. And we are. The time we lost was not your fault."

Candice closed her eyes briefly and squeezed Alex's hand as a silent gesture of appreciation and continued.

"Well, then, you don't have to pretend with me. I'm your family. And you can be in a lousy mood with your family…okay?"

"Okay," Alex said with a short sigh.

As they prepared to descend into Los Angeles, they held each other's hand to lend strength to the other as they both embarked on a new chapter in their lives.

"You know, I think that flight attendant had the hots for you, C.C."

Candice hadn't been called C.C. since she was in college. It made her feel good that Alex had so easily fallen back into their spirited camaraderie. The two women were a striking pair walking through the airport terminal, causing several men and ladies alike to take a second look and wonder who they were. This was L.A., and one never knew who they might see, especially in the airport. Alex was dressed in a yellow pencil skirt that fit her to a tee, matching pumps and a white French-cuffed cotton shirt that was unbuttoned to daringly show off a hint of cleavage. Her hair was pulled back in a beautiful gold clip, leaving it free to hang down her back, and she carried an exquisite leather briefcase that complemented her outfit. She was a small package, giving the impression she was ready for business or pleasure, and could easily have given Jada Pinkett Smith, the actress that matched her in size, a run for her money.

Candice, on the other hand, though not as thin as the supermodels were nowadays, was just as beautiful. Standing an entire ten inches above Alexandra, Candice was what men's fantasies were

145

made of: a beautiful appearance, a perfect shape, and legs for days. Her flawless brown face was framed by soft black curls that fell just past her shoulders. She walked with grace and precision, as if she were used to being on display. And even the simple grey sun dress she wore looked spectacular on her.

"What are you talking about?" Candice asked, pretending she was clueless about the comment Alex had made.

"You know exactly what I'm talking about," Alex responded, shooting a pointed look at Candice.

"Are you talking about the flight attendant that was old enough to be my dad?"

"Old enough, yes, but you have to admit he was very good looking…dad or not."

"If you say so, but the man was just doing his job. He's supposed to be nice, especially to the people forking out 'first class' money."

"If *you* say so," Alex said, smiling at Candice.

Having only hand luggage, they had no need to go to baggage claim. The car the firm had hired was waiting to take them to the hotel. Alex did not have to meet with the partners until the following morning. It was a Saturday, but it was the only day all the partners could be there to meet with her. Alex and Candice planned to spend the rest of the day sightseeing and shopping.

It was a perfect, cloudless day with a gentle breeze that hinted at endless possibilities. The weather was a far cry from the sweltering humidity of southern Louisiana. Alex could definitely get used to it. Candice and Alexandra were both practically hanging out of the windows like a couple of kids seeing an amusement park for the first time. They were pointing at buildings and landmarks they'd only before seen on television or heard about. By the time they reached the hotel, they were beaming with excitement and eager to drop off the bags and explore.

After unloading the bags, the driver informed Alex that the car service was at her disposal for the duration of her stay in Los Angeles. Alex thanked the driver and told him they would be ready to leave again in no more than thirty minutes. They checked in and found the law firm had taken care of all the details. The two women were hard pressed to contain the bubbling of excitement that threatened to spill over. The lobby of the Four Seasons was grandeur at its best, but they pulled themselves together, so as to not seem as if they weren't used to such sophisticated and luxurious surroundings.

Part of the lobby looked like it belonged in Buckingham Palace, with elegant sofas and tables so they could hardly wait to see what the room looked like. Alex had no idea what to tip a bellman. She hadn't ever had an opportunity to do so. There were only two small bags, but this was the Four Seasons after all, so she reached in her bag and handed the guy a twenty-dollar bill. His expression showed neither excitement at receiving a large tip nor disappointment at not receiving enough. He merely told them about some of the amenities of the hotel and wished them a pleasant stay.

There were two huge bouquets of roses on the table in the sitting room and a small gift basket on the desk.

"My goodness, Alex, they must really want you to work for them."

"I guess so," she said, walking over to the roses. She thought it was an odd choice of flowers for a prospective employee. There was a bouquet of yellow roses and a larger one in red.

The card on the red roses read: *A dozen roses for each day you've been in my life, Joshua.* Alexandra just stood there, reading the card over and over. Looking for some hint Joshua wanted more than those six days they'd known each other. Six days. Had it only been less than a week she'd known him? She reached for the other card on the yellow roses. There were a couple dozen of them. She was surprised and touched to see Candice's name on the card's envelope.

"These are for you, Candice." Alex handed her the card and saw confusion and a flash of fear cross her features.

"For me?" she said. "Who in the world knows I'm here?"

"Just open the card, C.C."

Alex gave her a reassuring smile and Candice reached to take the card from her. Candice looked at the flowers again, then read the card. She covered her mouth in disbelief and tears rolled from her eyes. The card read: *I thought you might need an extra helping of sunshine, Joshua Phoenix.*

"Oh, Alex, I know for sure you aren't doing fine." thinking of their conversation on the plane. "Joshua is pretty incredible, isn't he?"

"Yes, he is, C.C. Yes, he is…"

Chapter 17

Panic was an emotion Joshua Phoenix no longer had the luxury of expressing while being engulfed in the quicksand surrounding him. He was numb.

Is this how it was? Is this how people felt? Surefooted, on solid ground, then all of a sudden the earth you carelessly took for granted opens up and swallows you whole? You can't go back to find your solid footing again, because the effort may quicken your demise. You can't continue forward because everything you thought you were sure of changed the moment you saw her with her bags ready for the airport.

Joshua couldn't believe that after the night he and Alexandra had shared, she still wanted to go off without him. Their connection had been so primeval and soul-baring, he couldn't possibly see how he could continue through the course of his life as if he'd never known her. He had spent the entire night making love to her over and over, as if they couldn't get enough of each other. He didn't think he would ever be able to forget her face when they came together the very first time. There was something in her eyes that captivated him. Her lips had curved into a radiant and sure smile nestled between her adorable dimples that made her look angelic. And when he broke through the barrier confirming she'd never been touched by another man, the earth shifted. Time stood still. He knew he'd found a treasure more priceless than any the sea could hold. Alexandra Wyatt.

"Joshua?"

"What!" Joshua snapped, and immediately regretted it. A few people turned to look at the two men sitting together in the airport bar. Landon was limited to soda because he was flying out soon.

"Errrr. I suggest you put on the brakes, my brother, and back that train up," Landon Phoenix said, wondering what had gotten his brother into such a foul mood, but taking the time to notice the two women passing next to their table, practically licking their chops at him and Joshua. Joshua was dressed in a pair of jeans, a black t-shirt that did nothing to camouflage his well-chiseled chest and a tan sports coat. Landon was donned in his pilot's uniform, giving evidence as to why women loved men in uniform.

Due to the fact they didn't see each other much, they usually got along great. They were best friends as well as brothers, but lately Joshua had been somewhat unreachable and they hadn't had a chance to talk since the morning after the "Victoria incident". Landon had just so-happened to call Joshua before he turned off his cell phone after he was seated on his flight. They'd made arrangement to meet in New York during Joshua's layover and before Landon's flight back to London where he lived primarily.

No one would have ever guessed the two were brothers. They looked nothing alike, except they matched each other in height and were both well-built men. Both men were equally handsome, but other than that, they were like night and day. Joshua's skin was the color of smooth, rich chocolate, and Landon was nearly ivory in complexion. The older brother wore his hair cut close to his head, making him appear younger than his thirty-six years, and his brows and eyes formed a powerful team. He was the poster child for bedroom eyes. Most times they looked gray, but seemed to change with his mood and could easily appear a striking blue. Many a panty had literally fallen in defeat to the brow and eye duo, granting him the title of Quintessential Bachelor by those who knew him. Joshua and Landon did, however, have the same friendly smile or at least they started out the same, except somehow Landon's always turned into a mischievous grin. Their laughter, though, was identical.

"If I had known you were going to be in such a funky mood, I could have left earlier instead of hanging around New York so I could see you on your layover." He paused a moment and took a swallow of his drink. "Now, what the hell is wrong with you?"

"Sorry, man, I'm just tired. I didn't get much sleep last night and it was a long flight."

Joshua took a deep breath, rubbed his hand down his face and leaned back in his seat. The bar was loud and there was a basketball game on, drawing more people into the small establishment. Everyone was apparently in between flights, because the airport was crawling with travelers going to and fro. It was the last place he wanted to be.

"No sleep, huh? What's her name and better yet, does she have a sister?"

Joshua's lips thinned into an angry line and his features hardened. Landon was about to take another sip when he took a good look at his brother. Joshua literally looked as if his head was going to blow at any moment. Without taking his eyes off Joshua, he slowly placed his glass back on the table and leaned back heavily in his chair.

"Look, Josh…man, I was just messing around."

"Naw, that's okay… like I said, I'm tired and you know how grouchy I get when I'm tired."

"Umm, that's news to me. You're hardly ever grouchy. The last time I saw you in such a pissy mood was when…"

Landon stopped short when he saw the pain flash across Joshua's features.

"Aw man, say it ain't so?" Landon's brows furrowed and one corner of his mouth turned up in disgust as he stared across the table.

"It's so," Joshua said with a sigh of defeat.

Landon gripped his glass, sat back, and squinted with a fearful frown as if he were bracing himself for a punch in the face. He took another deep breath and finally said, "Just put me out of my misery, Josh. Is it Victoria Johnson?"

Joshua couldn't help but laugh. Landon always had a way of making him feel better, no matter what the circumstances. He'd done it to ease the tension between Joshua and their dad all his life.

"It's not Victoria Johnson. Do you think I'm insane?"

"Umm, am I under oath?" Landon thought it best not to mention that at one time it *had* been Victoria Johnson.

"Whatever man. Forget about it. It's over between Alexandra and me anyway." Joshua turned to look out at the people walking by.

"What's over?"

"You know, that's the funny part. I only met her last Saturday. We went out to dinner on Monday night, I was supposed to leave Tuesday morning and that would have been that. But noooo, like a fool I decided to hang around for a few days."

Landon didn't say a word. He just sat back and let Joshua talk.

"She'd just graduated from law school and I knew from the beginning...I knew from the beginning...and still like a fool..."

Their conversation was low enough for only the two of them to hear it, but Joshua was still working himself up into a ball of anger.

"You knew *what* from the beginning?" Landon asked, trying to refocus Joshua.

"I knew she would leave and go off to start her career without even taking a second glance back at me. I don't even think she wants to be a lawyer. It was a dream her father had for her before he died."

"Do you mean you offered her a chance to join you while you sail the seven seas or wherever you'll be on your new sailboat?"

Joshua paused a moment and scoffed at the incredulous statement."No..."

Before he could finish, Landon continued. "Oh, okay. So you recommended the two of you continue your 'relationship' on a long-distance basis for a while?"

Uneasiness was beginning to settle into the pit of Joshua's stomach. "No, I didn't." He barely mumbled like an insolent child.

"Okay. you expressed your undying love to her and she turned her back on you?"

Joshua felt like Candice was kicking *him* in the gut now. How could he be such an idiot? He didn't even respond to Landon. He just held his face in his hands.

"So, Joshua Kyle Phoenix, after only knowing this woman for six days, mind you; you are telling me that you offered this 'newly graduated to appease the dying wish of a father she loved' law student, nothing? Not even an expression of the love that you obviously seem to have? And what? You just expected her to relinquish the aspirations of a career she'd worked so hard for…for what, exactly?"

"Okay…okay… Landon, I get it. I've been an idiot."

"True," Landon said with a self-satisfied smile. "Alexandra, huh?"

"Yes, her name is Alexandra Wyatt," Joshua confessed with a heavy sigh.

"You know, Josh, I think you get some sort of perverse pleasure in sabotaging your own heart."

"What the hell do you mean by that?"

"You've fallen for two women in your entire life with your eyes wide open and somehow manage to seem surprised when it doesn't work out like you want it to."

Joshua was on the verge of protesting when Landon put his hand up to silence him. "Come on, Joshua, give me some credit here. You knew full well what type of person Victoria was from the start. She didn't turn into a power-seeking mongrel overnight; she was that way when we both met her. You just have this illusion that there's good in most people and deep down everyone has this warm, gooey, flowery feeling that love will conquer all and will be enough for them. Well, the truth, little brother, is that most people look out for what's best for them first and if love happens to accidentally fit into their particular purpose in life, then fine, but otherwise they could just as easily do without it. True love is something only found in books, movies and fairytales, anyway."

"If that's how you feel, Landon, then you're in worse shape than me."

"Why? Because I'm a realist? Look at yourself. You're a mess. You put off sailing on a boat you've spent forever going over every last detail to spend a few extra days with a woman that you don't even know if she has feelings for you or not. You can't concentrate and you clearly don't want to be sitting in this sports bar where the best game of the century is playing on the big screen so you can go off and pine alone for a woman who could probably care less about how you're doing."

Joshua took a drink of his beer and tried his best to reign in his anger before he spoke. He leaned over the table and looked directly at his brother. "You're not a realist, Landon. You're a coward."

The two brothers loved each other and had a great relationship, but though they were few, they had partaken in their share of no-holds-barred blowouts and this seemed to be one of those times. Landon narrowed his eyes at Joshua, waiting for him to continue.

"You're afraid to give your heart to someone, because you're scared as hell people will think you're like Dad," Joshua finished.

"What the hell does Dad have to do with any of this?"

"He has everything to do with your frivolous escapades with countless women and how you're turning into a callous bastard because of it."

Landon jumped to his feet, reached for his wallet and flung a few bills on the table. "Let's try this again when you're in a better mood," he spat out.

Joshua slammed his palms flat on the table and pushed himself up, glaring at his older sibling. Everyone in the bar, apart from them, was glued to the game, so no one paid any attention to the two engaged in the heated argument.

"Oh, it's okay to psychoanalyze everyone else, but when it's your turn to get on the sofa you turn tail and run? Sit down Landon!"

Landon's eyes seemed to throw off silver sparks as he held Joshua's gaze. He reluctantly took his seat and Joshua returned to his before continuing. "Don't you realize you are going out of your way to not be like our father?"

"Meaning?" Landon shot back.

"Meaning, you're trying to prove to him, yourself, or whomever, that you're never going to let a woman dictate your life the way Mom dictates Dad's. You're trying to prove you're more of a man than he is."

Landon shook his head and rolled his eyes, as if that were the most absurd thing he'd ever heard, but before Landon could speak, Joshua went on. "It's true and you know it. And I feel sorry for you."

Landon had had enough. He shoved his chair back and stormed over to Joshua who was rising from his seat as well. "You feel sorry for *me*! No one feels sorry for me! The person you should be feeling sorry for is the man who can't stand up to his wife. The man who lets his wife push him into favoring one son over the other because he happens to look more like the people whose asses they're always trying to kiss. That's who you should be feeling sorry for, Joshua...not for the brother that stood up for you, no matter what…"

Landon took a deep breath before he continued. "Now, like I said a few minutes ago, let's do this again when you're in a better mood. I have to fly to London in a half an hour."

Joshua watched Landon storm out of the sports bar, thinking about all those times Landon refused to be a part of any special activities if Joshua weren't included as well. It was times like those that made their relationship as strong as it was now. He knew it was hard for Landon to face the truth about his relationships, or the lack thereof, but he knew it was what his brother needed to hear in order for him to take ownership of his actions and realize he was more miserable than he claimed Joshua was at times.

Just as Joshua got up to leave, his cell phone rang. He looked at the number and wasn't surprised to see it was Landon. "Yeah?"

"Look, Josh, umm…" Landon paused a moment before continuing. "Well, I just didn't want to leave things as they were…"

Joshua knew Landon hated to argue with him and never liked to part on an angry note. He felt the same as well. "Landon, I have some loose ends to tie up before I set sail. I'll be in Boston for about a week

157

or so. Why don't you fly up and have a drink with me on my birthday, Tuesday? I promise to be in a better mood by then."

"Alright, Bro. You got a deal. Have a safe flight and I'll see you Tuesday."

"You too, Landon. I'll see ya soon." Joshua said a silent prayer he *would* be in a better mood by then and couldn't help wondering what Alexandra was doing or if she were thinking of him. In the same moment, he desperately prayed for the lifesaving rope to pull himself out from the sand he was sinking into.

Chapter 18

It wasn't exactly nervousness that Alexandra Wyatt felt as her heels clicked through the lobby of Coleman, Forrest and Twiggy. She was confident she could be a good lawyer, but she wondered if she lacked the passion she would need to become a great one. Her father had been one of the best environmental lawyers in the country. Other than his family, his life was the law. It was who Carl Wyatt was born to be. He lived for it and he spoke about it every chance he got. Not because he was consumed with work, but because he was consumed with passion for it. Alexandra hadn't thought about practicing law since she'd graduated one week ago. Not knowing what that meant is what had her a little apprehensive about her meeting with the partners.

The doors of the elevator closed, giving her a chance to look at her reflection. For a moment she didn't recognize the woman staring back at her. Her hair was pulled back and wound into a tight bun. She was wearing a grey pant suit with a white collared blouse and black pumps. She'd traded her pretty yellow briefcase she'd carried the day before for a serious black attaché case. Alexandra's appearance was very appropriate for her interview and her job, but what screamed back at her was dull, drab, and boring. Over the past few days she'd spent with Joshua, she'd learned how not to take life so seriously, but here she stood, as serious as they came.

The elevator doors parted, revealing a wall with the names Coleman, Forrest, and Twiggy, indicating she was on the correct floor. It was Saturday morning, but the entire floor was abuzz with activity. There were very few walls that weren't made of glass so she could see meetings going on around the massive mahogany tables with plush, black leather chairs. The occupants of most offices were clacking away at computers or poring through stacks of files on their desks.

Joshua's reasons for not subjecting himself to the corporate world came back to her. Instead of going to the beach, spending time with family, or just sleeping in, these people were here, at work, on a Saturday, as if it were the most normal thing in the world. Even if her father did work on Saturday, he did it from his office at home.

"Hello, I'm Alexandra Wyatt. I have an appointment with Mr. Coleman, Mr. Forrest, and Mr. Twiggy."

"Yes, ma'am. You're a few minutes early but you can wait for them in their private conference room."

The receptionist was in her late fifties with wiry, bright red hair that seemed oddly out of place in such a solemn environment. She was dressed professionally in a dark blue skirt and matching jacket, but still appeared to be out of her natural habitat. It could have been the dark pink blush she had smeared along her pale, white cheekbones or her drugstore press-on nails in a vivid shade of fuchsia. She looked like she should have been the receptionist at a retirement villa in South Florida instead of here in this prestigious law firm.

The private conference room was just as she stated, private. Its walls were a beautiful polished wood, lined with books. It was very similar to the magnificent libraries found in the homes of people with old money. There was, of course, a conference table like the others she'd seen, but there was also an area with sofas and chairs for more informal meetings. She was led to the sofa.

"May I get you some coffee or tea, Ms. Wyatt?" Red asked her after she placed her case down and took a seat.

"No, thank you, I'm fine," she said and immediately thought about the conversation she and Candice had on the plane about being "fine". She couldn't think of Joshua now. She needed to be able to concentrate on her interview.

Alexandra waited fifteen minutes before the partners were able to meet with her. The "interview" had turned out to be more of an orientation to the firm rather than a barrage of questions for her. They were obviously aware of her father's reputation, but assured her it was her own merit that made them take an interest in her. Her professors had given her glowing recommendations and they thought she would be a great fit with the firm. So basically all she had to do was decide if she would accept their offer, or not. The offer included a year's lease on a luxury condo and car until she established herself in L.A. and an enormous salary she was sure she would never have time to spend.

She politely thanked them for their generous offer and her accommodations at the Four Seasons.

161

They offered her a chance to stay through the next week to familiarize herself with the city, but she declined. She was honest with them, telling them of her interview in Boston. They were not surprised, knowing there would be many firms interested in her. She'd finished first in her class from a prominent environmental law program. They did however assure her no one would be able to match their great weather.

Spending the weekend in California with Candice had been just what the doctor ordered. Other than the few hours Alex had spent at the interview, she and Candice had absorbed as much of Los Angeles as they could. Aside from the scandalous prices, the shopping was downright therapeutic. Alex refused to look at the price tag until she had absolutely fallen in love with an outfit. She practically bought Candice a complete new wardrobe, about which she protested all the way, even after Alex told her about the money her father had left her upon graduation. Candice finally conceded when Alex nearly cried, begging Candice to let her do this for her. Shopping almost dulled the ache of missing Joshua.

It wasn't until nighttime came when the full onslaught of emotions struck her. She hadn't spoken to him since she'd left Baton Rouge and he didn't know she would even be in Boston. She wondered if he would be there or if he would have left for sailing by now. He had given her his address for the apartment he still kept in Boston and the number to the satellite phone on his sailboat, but she was hesitant to use either one.

She couldn't shake the idea that maybe he'd only given her his information and told her to call if she needed anything, out of obligation. He was after all, a gentleman. She'd known that the very first day when he gave her his jacket in the rain, not knowing if he would ever see her again to return it.

Waiting on the runway for nearly an hour to take off seemed to have only been about five minutes. She was anxious about going to Boston and plagued with the question of should she or should she not call Joshua when she got there.

"Do you think we will be able to call Joshua so I can thank him for the beautiful flowers?"

Alex could have sworn she heard cherubs singing "Hallelujah" somewhere in the distance. She loved Candice. Somehow she knew the inner turmoil she was dealing with and gave her perfect solution to save face.

"That shouldn't be a problem unless he's already left on his sailboat."

Alex tried to sound as nonchalant as she could and Candice only smiled as she continued to read her magazine. The plane at last started to ease along the runway. She was headed to Boston, where she hoped she would get to see Joshua.

Due to all the flight traffic, before the plane could start on its normal course, it had to make a wide loop. Alex couldn't understand how the sky could have some sort of traffic jam, but figured they knew what they were doing. Or at least she hoped they did. She didn't feel like reading the book she'd purchased for the flight, so she looked out the window instead.

What she saw nearly snatched her breath right from her chest. Never in her life had she seen anything that made her feel so free, so totally liberated. What she saw when she looked out the window was a firsthand view of the thing she'd come to love as a child. She looked down and with her own two eyes saw the edge of the United States. It was like looking at a map of California. She instinctively put her hand up to the window, trying to feel the bumps and ridges that comprised the mountains.

She could see the mighty Pacific Ocean rolling in, sweetly kissing the feet of the tiny dots of people along its shore. It made her want to be down there with them, enjoying it. She wanted to be in the car swerving up the mountain, smelling the salt air, getting a panoramic view of God's precious gift. It made her think of the people working on Saturdays and probably Sundays as well. It made her think of how she could very well be one of those people.

Alex could almost feel the wall closing in on her at the very thought of the near incarceration she would be subjecting herself to. And that's exactly what it would be to her, a form of incarceration, because she lacked the passion for it. Looking down below, she felt the excitement she'd always felt as a girl, dreaming of the exciting places she would experience, and she also felt the choking sensation of being incased behind the glass walls of the law firm; oblivious to anything beyond her surroundings.

"Candice, if money were no object, would you still be an artist?"

"I would have to say, yes. It's who I am; even if no one else liked what I did, I would still have to do it for me." She paused a moment before she continued. "Being able to paint again saved my life."

Alex instinctively reached for Candice's hand.

"What about you Alex? Is being a lawyer who you really are?" Alex turned away, still unsure of the answer to that question.

"It's what my father always wanted for me."

"But what do *you* want Alex?" Candice gently tugged Alex's arm so she would look at her.

"I want to make my daddy proud," she whispered.

"You are a beautiful, intelligent woman. You are kind and caring. You know right from wrong. You are strong and determined. Alexandra Wyatt, I am positive you father is beyond proud of his little girl."

Alex couldn't help the small tear that spilled over her lid.

"But he wanted me to be a lawyer like him."

"Yes, but more importantly, he wanted what was best for you. And if not being a lawyer is best for you, Al, then that's what he would want for you. He wanted you to be happy. Do you really think your father would want you to just go through the motions of a job he loved? It would be like a slap in the face to him."

Alex hadn't thought of it that way before. Her father had no respect for attorneys that were in it just for the money or the recognition.

"Candice Freedman, I love you. You are absolutely what I need right now." Alex reached over and gave her friend a hug.

"I love you too, Alex, but I think what you need is to talk to Joshua."

Alex just leaned her head back and closed her eyes. She wasn't ready to admit to Candice how much she really needed to talk to and see Joshua. She hadn't really wanted to admit it to herself. Would he be glad to hear from her, or would he be annoyed she had actually called him? He hadn't even bothered to ask where she would be going after she left California. Maybe he didn't care. These were the thoughts that danced around in her head, preventing her from sleeping.

When she allowed herself to be honest in her musings, it was hard for her to imagine that the Joshua Phoenix she'd come to know and love would be anything but sincere. She refused to believe the intimacy they'd shared that last night meant nothing to him, and was determined he knew how much it meant to her.

Chapter 19

The long flight left them both exhausted. Meandering through the crowd, Candice and Alexandra wished they had the convenience of bypassing the baggage claim area again, but of course their marathon shopping spree in L.A., and even Beverly Hills, prevented it. They both ended up with a carry-on, two checked bags, plus two more bags they had to pay a hundred bucks a pop to check.

The smell of delicious coffee beans lured Alex. She would kill for a White Chocolate Mocha from Starbucks, so she could at least stay awake until they made it to the hotel. The line was long, but it was of course worth it. The wait went rather quickly and it wasn't long before their names were called to pick up the coffee at the other end of the counter. Alex picked up her coffee and before she could get the coveted liquid to her lips, she turned around and collided with the next customer.

He turned out to be a real sport about the entire incident and even insisted on buying her another cup. When he ordered two more coffees, they didn't charge him, seeing that it was an accident. Had she not been so tired, she would have been mortified, but fatigue, she guessed, lessened shame.

The man asked the guys behind the counter to hold his coffee while he made a quick change of his shirt. Luckily, he was a pilot, so he had his suitcase with him. Alex had gotten coffee on the jacket of the casual suit she was wearing, but she had just removed it. She asked the guy behind the counter for the pilot's coffee, along with her own, when they were ready. She was going to wait for him near the bathroom so he wouldn't have to go back into the crowded coffee shop.

When he walked out of the bathroom freshly changed into a pair of jeans and pullover shirt, she, and apparently several other women, noticed how incredibly handsome he was. One woman dared to stop in his path to give him a once-over, from head to toe. He gave the bold vixen an appreciative grin and turned his attention to the two women waiting with his coffee. He approached Alex and Candice with an easy smile, but his gaze, Alex noticed, lingered on Candice a few seconds longer than necessary. She dismissed the notion of his smile being oddly familiar as she handed him his coffee, looking very apologetic.

"You didn't have to wait for me. I would have gotten it when I came out." He was glad she had, though; the woman with her was gorgeous. "Do you have another flight to catch?" he asked, hoping they didn't.

"No, we're visiting Boston for a few days so this is our stop. I just couldn't leave without apologizing again and making sure the coffee didn't burn you."

"There's no apology necessary. It was an accident, and the best thing about Starbucks coffee is that it's always the perfect temperature."

"Yeah, but the perfect temperature is still hot. Are you sure you're okay?"

"Never better," he said, glancing over at Candice.

"Well, I'm glad," she said and awarded him her traffic-stopping smile. "Please, don't let us keep you. You must have a flight to get to."

He was almost knocked off balance by her radiant, dimpled smile and was in no hurry to depart the company of the two strikingly beautiful women. "Actually, this is my stop as well. I flew in on my normal route from London to New York, then had the luxury of being a passenger on the flight here. By the way, my name is Landon." He reached out his hand to Alex first.

"Nice to meet you, Landon, I'm Alexandra Wyatt, and this is my friend, Candice Freedman."

Where her smile had failed, her introduction finished the job. He was too stunned for words, but recovered nicely.

"Would the two of you like to join me while we enjoy our coffee?" he asked, not taking his eyes off of Candice. Something about this man made Alex feel she'd met him before, but that couldn't be possible. He was very handsome and his striking, gray eyes were almost seductive in a way, but it wasn't attraction she was feeling. It was as if she were missing something right in front of her.

"We've already taken up too much of your time; besides we need to pick up our luggage."

"Oh, they'll hold it for you until you get there. C'mon, it's the least you can do, seeing that you poured hot coffee all over me." His eyes glittered with playfulness. "What do you think, Candice?"

Breaking the hold Landon seemed to have on her gaze, she turned to Alex. "I agree. It's the least we can do." Then turned back to Landon, "You could have been scarred with second-degree burns because of her." Candice's lips curved into a shy smile, unbelieving that she could be taken in so easily by this natural-born charmer.

Alex couldn't believe it, either. Candice had been almost withdrawn when she came in contact with men while they were in L.A. Now she was voluntarily placing herself in the presence of a man she didn't even know.

"Well, I guess when you put it that way, I have no other choice," Alexandra conceded.

The trio sat, drinking and talking easily about their flights, what it was like to fly back and forth to London, and things they should see and do in Boston. They talked like old friends for nearly an hour, and anyone passing by would have thought they'd known each other for years. This was the first man Alex had seen Candice comfortable around since Joshua. Joshua!

Alex stared at Landon, looking for some similarity, and realized she'd noticed it from the beginning, but hadn't put two and two together since this man was nearly white. Landon had been discussing with Candice some of the art museums he'd visited in Paris when he noticed Alexandra staring at him. Candice turned to look at Alex as well, wondering what was causing her friend to be so rude. Landon was sure she had finally figured it out and again gave her the smile she'd recently become familiar with. There it is, she thought. It's the exact same smile she'd been dreaming about since the last time she saw Joshua.

"Is something wrong, Alexandra?" he asked knowingly.

"Landon!" she almost barked.

"Yes?" he said, with that same smile but the corner of it turned into something more. Something that told her he'd known who she was all along.

"Landon…as in Landon Phoenix?" She saw Candice's mouth grow slightly agape when she added the last part.

"The one and only." The grin on his face made his eyes dance wildly.

"Landon Phoenix, brother of Joshua Phoenix?" She knew it, but just wanted to be absolutely certain.

"You're Joshua's brother?" Candice asked in amazement.

"Yes, I am," he said, first to Candice, then he looked at Alex. "I didn't mention it at first because I didn't know if that would make or break my chances of sharing my coffee with you two."

Alex just looked at him, not sure what to say to the comment he'd just made. He took advantage of her silence and continued. "So now that all the introductions are out of the way, and you two know I'm not some sort of lunatic or something..."

"That remains to be seen," Alex broke in.

Landon liked her already. His hearty laughter was infectious and broke the slight tension. "Like I was saying before I was rudely interrupted," he looked pointedly at Alex, feeling comfortable with her now, "even though my lunacy is in question, how about I give you two a ride to your hotel?"

Could she really impose on Joshua's brother this way? How would he feel about her showing up in Boston and soliciting a ride from Landon? She did want to see him and it was an absolute certainty his

171

*brother would tell him she was in town. It had all been
an accident how they met and it would be convenient
not to have to get a cab with all the luggage, but it
wasn't just up to her.*

"Candice?" Alex gently asked, touching her
forearm.

"I think it's a wonderful idea, but we have lots
of luggage," she said, turning to Landon, looking very
sheepish, wondering if that would break the deal, but
hoping it didn't. She was really enjoying Landon's
company and hearing about all the places she dreamed
of going.

"That shouldn't be a problem. I always rent an
SUV, anyway." He couldn't help but wonder what
Joshua would think of the birthday gift he was bringing
him.

"So, Alexandra, Joshua tells me you just
completed law school." Landon was looking at Alex
through the rearview mirror as they made their way
from the airport. It was decided that since Candice
needed more leg room, she would sit in front with
Landon. He was trying to get a feel for how she felt
about Joshua.

"Yes, that's right," she said, staring out the
window at nothing in particular. Her stomach was in
knots.

"And you had an interview in California?"

"Umm huh."

"So how did it go, if you don't mind me
asking?" This was like pulling teeth, he thought.

"It went rather well, but I haven't given them a
decision yet." She turned to look at him, "I didn't think

it was fair to them or me to make a decision without interviewing with the other firm. That's why I'm here."

Alex was trying to make clear her reasons for being in town. She wondered what other things Joshua had mentioned to him.

"Well, that sounds logical. Hey, how about if we go grab some dinner after you check in to your hotel?"

Alex was sure she wouldn't be able to eat a thing, knowing she was in the same city as Joshua. She'd already made it a point not to ask Landon anything about him besides asking how he was doing. "Maybe another time; I'm beat," she lied.

"Well, how about you, Candice? We could grab something at the hotel if you want." His voice was so low and enticing, Alex was sure he was scaring Candice to death. Just as she was about to make up some excuse for her, Candice spoke up.

"I am kind of hungry. Are you sure you don't mind?" Candice replied a little timidly.

"It will be my pleasure. Plus you'll be saving me from eating alone or eating at my parents' house."

"Then it's settled," she said, feeling a little giddy. "Alex, are you sure you don't want to join us?" Alex studied her friend, looking for some hint Candice wanted her to get her out of this, but Candice looked excited about her meal with Landon.

"Are you okay, Candice? You look as if you're expecting someone." He'd noticed her looking over her shoulder every few minutes after they were seated.

173

"To be perfectly honest with you, Landon, you're the first man other than my husband and father I've been alone with in quite some time."

"So you're married? I didn't see a ring, but if you're uncomfortable, I'll understand." He did his best to hide the disappointment in his voice. Which was a little disconcerting to him, because he'd never really cared enough about any woman to be disappointed by them. Yet he regretted finding out Candice was married.

"Yes, I'm married, but there is no ring because I've recently left my husband." She absently rubbed the spot where the ring used to be. "That's the first time I've said that out loud… I've left my husband." She said it again, as if she really couldn't believe it was true. She leaned in closer, placed her hand over her chest and smiled. "I've left my husband."

Landon just sat there, watching her little drama unfold with a raised eyebrow. "Ooohkay," he said, as if he'd just realized she was nuts. Candice looked up at him, momentarily forgetting he was there. "I'm sorry, Landon. I know I must sound like a lunatic , but just this very moment it hit me that I'm truly free. And as far as being uncomfortable; this is the first time I've been comfortable with a man besides my father."

"And your husband…right?"

"Wrong," she uttered, unable to look at him.

"I don't mean to get into your business, Candice, but was he a slob in public or something?" he said jokingly. "I mean, usually the only time women are uncomfortable around their husbands is when they are abusive to them."

The moment the words slipped from his mouth, he saw the pain and shame cloud her features. He felt like an ass, but it was impossible for him to imagine anyone putting their hands on Candice except to thoroughly make love to her.

"I'm sorry, Landon, maybe this was a mistake. I shouldn't be here." She couldn't even look at him and it clawed at his gut, knowing he'd caused her to feel that way. He reached across the table and grabbed her hand. He could feel it tremble, making him mad as hell that someone of his species felt he had the right to hurt her.

"Don't go, Candice. I'm the one who's sorry. I shouldn't have said that."

"It's not your fault. All you wanted was dinner and here I am laying this soap opera on the table." She wanted to get up and walk away, but his gaze held her rooted to her spot.

"It's not your fault, either," he said gently

Closing her eyes, she turned her head away. "It's taken a long time for me to realize that…" Looking at him again, she added, "and I'm still not sure that I fully do."

"It's not your fault, Candice," he said again, still holding on to her hand.

She wanted to believe him, but she'd spent years hearing otherwise and she wasn't sure how long it was going to take to convince her to believe it.

Chapter 20

"Landon called. He said he was bringing a couple of guests to Joshua's party." Jocelyn Phoenix told her husband. She was looking at him from the reflection in her vanity mirror while she completed her nightly ritual of brushing her hair. It was a silky jet black with just a few grey strands she allowed to show, to give her a more distinguished matronly look. She was, after all, the mother of two grown sons although they had yet to give her any grandchildren.

The nightly routine of the couple never changed. After they emerged from their separate bathrooms, Dixon donned in his silk pajamas and Jocelyn in what was sure to be some very expensive and exquisite lounging attire, he retired to the bed with a book and reading glasses while Jocelyn sat at the antique vanity and brushed her hair.

"That's nice. I'm surprised you were able to talk Joshua into having a party in the first place" Her husband absently replied.

"That's nice?" she repeated as she turned to face him. "That's nice?... Is that all you can say about your son ruining his life."

Dixon Phoenix was busily trying to prop himself up comfortable in bed with a book when his wife's words reached him. "Ruining his life? I thought we were just talking about him bringing a couple of guests to the party. Are they terrorists or something?" he chuckled, trying to keep his wife's hackles down. It didn't work.

"They may as well be. You know how superficial Landon is when it comes to women. All that matters to him is that she's beautiful."

"And what's wrong with dating a beautiful woman? Besides he says he's bringing two guests. What makes you think they are his dates?"

"Give me a break Dixon; you know our son as well as I do. He'll soon be over this 'pilot thing' and will need to be on the right track for real success. It's our job to make sure all the best opportunities are available to him. He'll need to have a wife at his side that can secure him a place in proper society."

"And just what kind of wife is that?" he asked, feeling the familiar pangs of annoyance.

Instead of answering him, Jocelyn turned back to the mirror to deftly twine her hair into the single braid that held it taut every night. When she'd made sure every hair was in place, she slowly turned to face her husband again.

"The kind of wife that knows what their husband and sons need to be successful in privileged society."

Dixon placed his book down and scooted his glasses further down on the bridge of his nose, peering at his wife over the rim of them. "I thought it was our job to make sure our children grew up happy, healthy and responsible."

"You see…men like you, need women like me. Wasn't it I who encouraged you to take over your first company? That bold move was the initiation to other takeovers. Without my influences with some of the most powerful families in Boston, none of it would have been possible." Jocelyn stood and walked to the bed with a self-satisfied smile as if she'd just told him she'd partnered with God in the Creation. "Now *we're* one of the most influential families in Boston and with Landon's charm and looks, his possibilities are endless."

"What about Joshua and his possibilities." Dixon had heard it all before; his wife puffing herself up as if they would have been destitute if it had not been for her. He also was sick to death of her making differences between their sons. What was even worse was that he allowed himself to go along with her. "And I don't recall you lacking for anything before I started acquiring and selling companies. The more money we made, the more estranged my sons became to me. I was just grateful Cortland was there to spend time with them."

"Yes that was beneficial to us wasn't it? With their dark coloring, many people believed Joshua was Cortland's son and we were raising him because Cortland had no wife. Explaining Cortland as your brother was a bit more difficult."

Dixon Phoenix was incredulous. His face showed the anxiety his mind was going through. He often felt his wife was biased towards Landon, because he was so fair skinned. But to come right out and admit she was glad people may have thought Joshua was the son of his brother left a foul taste in his mouth.

"How did your parents explain Cortland to people anyway?" she asked, oblivious to the horrid look being directed at her.

"How did they explain him?" he sputtered as he sprang from the bed. "How in the hell do you explain your callous attitude towards your own flesh and blood!" He shook inside with rage and shame for all the years he'd let her foster differences between Landon and Joshua. He was just grateful the two brothers had remained close no matter what.

"Dixon, how dare you speak to me in that tone?" she asked barely raising her voice; maintaining her staunch decorum.

"How dare I? You've got to be kidding me. You've just all but admitted you wished Joshua wasn't our son, because his skin happens to be darker than ours."

"I did no such thing."

"How could I have been so blind all these years?" he asked almost to himself. "How could I have let you infect this family with your prejudice venom?"

"Dixon, get back in bed. You're working yourself into a thither for nothing." Jocelyn smoothed down her comforter and straightened her pillow. "Be a dear will you, and hand me my sleep mask from my vanity."

It was as if a rocket had gone off in his head and all his senses had come alive. "Get your own damn mask. I'm sleeping in one of the guest rooms." He turned towards the door and thought better of it. Dixon walked back around to his wife's side of the bed and stood over her. "For your information my brother wasn't some bastard child we were hiding in the basement. He was an equal member of our family that we all loved. It was no secret that my grandmother was a black woman and there was no shame that when Cortland was born his coloring resembled hers. My parents loved us and treated us the same." Dixon was trembling as he spoke, but not from fear of berating his

179

wife to her face; trying to contain his rage shook him to the core. He leaned in close to her face so there would be no doubts in what he wanted to say and through gritted teeth, he told her exactly what he should have years ago, "I am ashamed of how I've allowed you to treat Joshua. No more my dear, no more" He stood to leave, but before he turned to walk away he glowered at her, "your influence over me is over Jocelyn and I'm not about to let you do to our sons, what you've done to me."

Jocelyn was stunned. She was visibly shaken. Her husband had never spoken to her that way before. Of course they've had minor disagreements in the past, but he had never raised his voice to her. Didn't he understand that things may have looked as if they'd changed over the years, but essentially it was still a white man's world? Why should she feel guilty for being privileged to be born to very fair skinned blacks? It wasn't her fault that white people still seemed to think very light skinned blacks had a better pedigree, therefore was more worthy to associate with. Didn't she do her best to make sure Joshua went to good schools and dated worthy women? Hadn't it been *her* that encouraged Victoria to give him another chance so he wouldn't waste his life sailing around with no future? Jocelyn felt all her actions had been justified, but as she looked over at the empty space beside her she felt a tremor; of what, she wasn't sure.

Dixon settled into the bed in the guest room and enjoyed the most peaceful night of sleep he'd ever had.

Chapter 21

"Okay, Greg, sounds great. Okay....I told you, I've already thought about it...Yes, now go take care of your wife...Okay, talk to you soon." Alex ended her call with Greg and turned her attention back to Candice.

"We're what?" Alex said, looking at Candice, who was standing over her bed looking through all four of her suitcases.

"You heard me. We were invited to a birthday party," Candice answered without looking up at Alex.

"Whose birthday party?" Alex asked, not hiding her agitation.

"Joshua's." Candice looked up at her. "You'd better hurry and get dressed; Landon will be here in about an hour," she said casually.

"Candice Paulette Carwin, what do you mean Landon will be here in an hour!" her voice rising, unable to believe what she was hearing.

"Just what I said, Alex. Today is Joshua's birthday, his parents are giving him a little dinner party, and Landon insisted we attend."

She failed to mention that she and Landon thought this would be the perfect opportunity for the couple to get their act together. Candice looked up at Alex again. "Aren't you going to shower?"

Alexandra let out a frustrated squeal and stomped off to the bathroom. Candice sat on the bed in a fit of laughter when she heard the bathroom door slam.

Alex sat in the backseat of Landon's SUV, wishing she had a slingshot to pop Landon and Candice both in the back of the head with something. They sat in the front, comfortably talking and being all chummy, while she sat in the back, feeling like her stomach was turned inside out. She didn't even know if Joshua knew she was coming, or not.

"Landon, is Joshua expecting us? I mean, I would hate to crash his party."

Landon looked back at her through the mirror and answered, "It's a surprise, so he isn't expecting anyone."

She looked out the window again, oblivious to the cars passing and people walking along the sidewalks. *Great, she thought. Just great.*

Candice glanced back at Alex, then gave Landon a mischievous smile.

The small dinner party was more like a grand gala. There were about one hundred fifty people in attendance. Alex had no idea how this was supposed to be a surprise party with valets out front and a live band you could hear from blocks away. When she entered the home, she saw it was very elegant but lacked a sense of warmth. It looked much more like a museum than a home. There was expensive furniture throughout, but nothing cozy enough to lounge on during cold winter nights. She wondered where Mr. and Mrs. Phoenix sat together to watch a movie and eat popcorn or if they did at all. There were vases in every nook and cranny and little knickknacks everywhere. Somehow she couldn't imagine children living there, running and playing on the pricey rugs and furniture.

The entire image fit neither Joshua nor Landon's personality. The party, she noticed, was being held behind the house in a beautiful courtyard illuminated by thousands of tiny, white lights. Mrs. Phoenix obviously spared no expense for her son's birthday party.

The moment the three of them stepped into the courtyard, a handsome couple came to greet them. The woman was petite and wore a champagne-colored cocktail dress with a scooped neck and high waist that flared into an a-line, stopping at the knees. She looked very elegant, but her flawless, pale face was hard and serious. Her hair, Alex noticed, was pulled back in a severe bun, like she'd worn hers until meeting Joshua.

My goodness, do I look as cold as she does when I wear my hair like that? Are these Joshua and Landon's parents?

The woman looked passé blanc, as a Creole would say in Louisiana. She could easily have passed for white in Alex's great grandmother's days. If the man with her was their father, she realized then how Joshua had ended up with such silky locks, but from whom he had inherited his magnificent dark coloring, she had no idea. His father looked white, and if he wasn't, she was sure one of his parents had been. He was incredibly handsome and looked striking in a pair of tan chinos and a cream-colored sports coat.

"Landon, it's so kind of you to finally grace us with your presence. And who are your dates?"

"Mom, please...Behave…And they are not my dates. This…" he said, referring to Alex, "is Alexandra Wyatt, a friend of Joshua's from Louisiana."

That last bit of news caused the woman to lift an eyebrow and look Alex up and down like she was some indigent off the streets. "And this is her friend, Candice Freedman. They are in town for a few days."

"Is that so?" the older woman asked with suspicion.

"And ladies...this enchanting creature is my mother, Jocelyn Phoenix..." His sarcasm didn't go unnoticed by his mother. Her face seemed to harden even more; if that was even possible. "...and my father, Dixon Phoenix."

"How lovely to meet you Alex and Candice," he said as he shook each lady's hand ignoring his wife's dirty look. "I'm sure Joshua will be glad to see faces he recognizes. He always hates these little functions his mother insists on throwing."

"It's nice to meet you," they both seemed to say at the same time. Alex noticed the look Jocelyn shot her husband and she also noticed the stunned expression Landon had on *his* face. Landon didn't know what to make of his father at the moment. He could almost believe his father purposely welcomed Alex and Candice so warmly just to irritate his mother.

Before mingling with the crowd, Alex asked Landon to show her to the bathroom. Just like the other parts of the home she'd seen, the guest bathroom was a showplace for elegance. As she ventured back through the hallway to the party, she stopped to look at the pictures on the wall. Alex couldn't help smiling at seeing the two brothers as young boys. One of the pictures featured Joshua grinning widely at a small sailboat, hugging a tall, handsome man that looked like his father, but was as dark as Joshua. That, she thought, must be his Uncle Cortland. Dixon Phoenix and Cortland were an older version of Landon and Joshua. Alex had never asked Joshua about his family history, but was convinced it must be an interesting one. As she glanced at the other pictures, she noticed the only pictures in which Joshua smiled, were those of only him and Landon or those with his Uncle Cortland.

Alex hurried back to the party with Landon and Candice. Landon left the two women standing near the bar, so he could find Joshua before he found them. Alex was sure this was no surprise party and hoped the surprise didn't somehow turn out to be on her. She looked around, trying to see if she could spot Joshua, but the birthday boy didn't seem to be anywhere to be found.

"I'm sure he'll be around soon," Candice said, taking a sip of her wine.

"What the hell are we doing here, Candice?"

"Umm… language!"

"Don't look now, but here comes Mrs. Phoenix," Alex whispered

"Where? Oh, I see her. Who do you think that woman is with her?"

Alex looked closely. Though she'd only gotten a glimpse of her that night in New Orleans, she would have recognized Victoria anywhere.

"That, my friend, is Joshua's ex-fiancée."

"You don't say."

"I do say," she whispered as the two women approached. Victoria was maybe a few inches shorter than Candice with a pale pasty face and lacking any womanly curves. She looked like string cheese in a

185

cocktail dress that was obviously tailored to fit her none figure. Alex wondered if the woman even knew what a carb tasted like.

"Oh, there you are, dear. I wanted you to meet Joshua's fiancée. They haven't made an official announcement yet, but we know it will be coming soon." Jocelyn was beaming at Victoria with pride.

"Is that right?" Alex said, smiling sweetly.

What in the world was keeping Landon? He should have been here two hours ago. Joshua was sitting in the kitchen, knowing no one would find him in there. The only people that came in the kitchen were the caterers and the kitchen staff. How he'd let his mother talk him into having this party was beyond him. She'd even had the audacity to invite Victoria and he'd even overheard his mother introducing her as his fiancée. If Landon didn't show up in the next five minutes, he was out of there.

"Sorry it took me so long, man," Landon said as he entered the kitchen. "I had to pick up your present and it wasn't ready when I got there," referring to the extra half hour he had to wait for Alex to get ready. He and Candice had sat in the lobby, enjoying each other's company while they waited.

"Apology not accepted. No present is worth this kind of torture. Let's get out of here," Joshua grumbled.

"Wait! I need to get the present first," Landon said, walking towards the courtyard.

"No…no…hell no! I'm not going back in there in a crowd of uptight, phony people that I don't even know, celebrating *my* birthday."

186

"C'mon, Josh, I had to pick it up from the airport."

Landon was giving him a pitiful face and managed to get him as far as the entrance of the courtyard.

"There it is, over there," he said, pointing in the direction of where he'd left the two women. "Aw shit!" Landon exclaimed.

Joshua looked in the area where Landon had pointed. He hadn't been drinking so he knew he wasn't drunk and seeing things. He grabbed Landon's arm before he could escape.

"Is that…is that…Alexandra?" Joshua was momentarily stunned.

"Umm, yeah, man, happy birthday, but if we don't get over there now, there's no telling what Mom and the wicked witch are telling her."

"What's she doing here? How did she…?"

"I'll explain it all to you later; now let's get over there."

Alexandra didn't know how much more of the "Victoria Tales" she could take.

"Victoria, weren't you in New Orleans recently to visit with Joshua?" the older woman asked.

"Yes, ma'am, briefly," Victoria confirmed in a voice barely audible. She obviously remembered it wasn't a very pleasant experience. Alex almost felt sorry for her. Almost.

"Oh, did the two of you get a chance to meet? Being a friend of Joshua's and all, I would think you'd had the opportunity to be at the same functions," Mrs. Phoenix asked them. The woman obviously did not know the circumstances surrounding the event, but

187

Alex was fed up with her trying to shove Victoria in her face.

"Oh, right…the hotel room…. was that you?" Alex asked sweetly. "As a matter of fact, I thought you looked familiar. I'm sorry, at the time I thought you were a stripper who had finagled her way into the wrong room. My mistake."

With that, Alex turned on her heels and walked away, leaving Mama Phoenix and her precious Victoria unable to close their mouths. When Alex turned, she found herself face to face with a smiling Joshua.

Landon was beside himself. "Alexandra Wyatt, I think I love you!" he said, picking her up and spinning her around. "No one has had the nerve to put those two in their place in years." His zesty grin was short lived when he got a look at Joshua's grim features. He guessed that Joshua didn't take too kindly to another man telling his girl he loved her. He quickly gathered Candice by the waist and led her to the dance floor.

"Happy birthday," she whispered, unable to breathe at a steady pace.

Joshua looked at Candice and Landon, dancing as if they'd known each other for years, then looked back down at Alex. "Whatever magic transpired to get you here, I don't even want to know or even care how it happened; all I know is that I'm glad you're here."

"You are?"

"Yes, I am, and if you don't mind, I'd like to show you how glad I am."

"I don't mind," she whispered.

That was all he needed to hear before he leaned over and claimed her mouth as his. Her body immediately recognized the source of its great pleasure recently and molded into his. They poured all their longing, needs, and love into that kiss, not caring who saw or what they thought. Joshua came to his senses first; realizing they needed to get out of there, and fast.

As Landon and Candice exited the dance floor, he saw his mother and Victoria still glued to the spot where Alex had left them gawking. His eyes danced with delight as he gave them a smile the Cheshire Cat would be envious of.

"Oh the love of springtime. Isn't it great?"

They both glared at him as he laughed and walked away.

"Hey, you two, I suggest you find somewhere else to do that. You're going to give these snooty old geezers a heart attack. Let's say you, me, Candice and Al here, get out of here and go have some real fun."

Still holding Candice at the waist, the couple walked towards the house.

"Al?" Joshua asked with a questioning expression.

"Long story…" she answered, looking up at him. "I think we were set up," she confessed as she nodded towards her friend and his brother walking ahead of them.

"I think you're right and I would like to hear this long story. But right now, we'd better get out of here before their evil stares disintegrate us."

Joshua raised an eyebrow and nodded in the direction of his mother and Victoria, who were still standing there in stunned silence. He held Alex tightly, unable to believe she was really there with him. No one saw Dixon Phoenix standing off to the side silently cheering on Alex for standing up to Jocelyn. She must be something special he thought, as he watched his son walk away with Alex with a twinge of envy of their apparent happiness.

Epilogue

Nothing enhanced the start of a perfect evening better than watching the sun slip beneath the horizon from the deck of *The Phoenix*. Alex was still impressed with the massive size and exquisite beauty of the yacht. Calling it a sailboat somehow didn't do justice to the vessel. The moment she saw it, she knew she'd found a new love. Joshua was more than thrilled that Alex took to sailing like a fish to water.

Of course, she'd seen the sun set countless times while she and Joshua were out sailing, but today it was more spectacular than usual. As a matter of fact, the ocean smelled a little sweeter, the cloudless sky was a little bluer and though just yesterday she had felt as if she couldn't possibly love Joshua any more, today she did. Two months ago to the day, she didn't even know Joshua's last name, but today he not only shared his name with her, he had pledged to share his life and love as well.

Neither had wanted to taint their special day with people who weren't genuinely happy for them. So they'd opted out of the elaborate wedding Jocelyn Phoenix insisted on planning. She had grudgingly accepted Alexandra as Joshua's fiancée, but still regarded her as if she were a second-class citizen and was none too pleased with their decision for a small private ceremony with only family. She'd even gone so far as to pick out Alex's wedding gown. Much to Joshua's surprise, his father had welcomed Alex into the family without qualms and had openly disagreed with his mother about the wedding plans and made a genuine effort in being more involved in his life. He'd even been out sailing with Joshua a couple of times which nearly left Landon speechless when Joshua told him about it. It was difficult to try to overcome years of his father being absent in his life, but with Alexandra's encouragement he was trying.

Tired of Jocelyn Phoenix's uninvited involvement, they planned a private wedding on *The Phoenix* with only Landon as the best man and Candice to stand beside Alex. Joshua invited his father, but Dixon didn't want to cause any undue awkwardness at his son's wedding and encouraged him to go ahead with his original plans of only having Landon and Candice. The two had not seen each other since their initial meeting in Boston, but Landon checked on Candice often, providing invaluable support and friendship as she started divorce proceedings from her husband. Her parents had been shocked when she told them of the abuse, but even more saddened at the thought that their daughter had been living in hell and they hadn't suspected a thing.

Of course, Lillian Carwin had jumped into action by making sure Candice got the counseling she needed and had encouraged her to join a support group with other battered women. Candice seemed to be handling her newfound independence well. She had a small home and had completed a second collection of artwork. Alex and Joshua had viewed and bought a few more pieces from her new collection when they flew to Louisiana to sign some paperwork for the bar Alex now co-owned.

Greg had refused to accept the loan from Alex to rebuild the bar unless she became co-owner. She'd made the decision during her flight to Boston not to pursue her father's dream of working with a law firm. She found she actually enjoyed being a business owner. Her intention was to be a silent partner, but Greg would have none of that. She'd actually made several suggestions that would eventually be very beneficial to the bar. She was even toying with the idea of opening a coffee house in the Boston area or in one of the ports they often visited. She and Joshua both thought it would be very cost-effective if their future businesses had their own "in-house" lawyer, so Alex decided to study for the Louisiana bar exam.

"What are you thinking about, Mrs. Phoenix?" Joshua asked, holding his wife firmly from behind as the sun made its final bow of the evening.

"I was thinking of how much I felt my dad's presence today."

"You aren't sad, are you?"

"How could I be? Surrounded by the two people that mean the most to us, you officially became my dream come true." With his arms still holding her securely to him, Alex turned to face her husband. "I'm sure my dad was letting me know how proud he was of me, knowing how happy I am."

"Are you truly happy, Alex? I know most women want all the bells and whistles for their wedding day. All you got was a simple ceremony on a sailboat."

He looked so serious, she wanted to wrap herself around him and show him just how happy she was, but instead she smiled back sweetly and answered him.

"Wasn't it you, Joshua Phoenix, who told me I needed to enjoy the simple pleasures in life?"

"I believe I did."

"And wasn't it you too, Joshua Phoenix, who told me not to take life too seriously?"

"Yes, that would be me as well."

"Then how in the world could I not be happy with a wedding that saved me from hours and hours of being able to do this?"

She reached up to wrap her arms around his neck, unable to put off the wedding night any longer. Just as he always did, he instinctively lifted her off the deck and cupped her bottom. He was glad her dress didn't restrict her legs from clutching him around the waist. He was also glad Candice and Landon, along with the minister, had left immediately after the ceremony on a sailboat Landon had rented for the occasion. Briefly, Joshua wondered about the pair and the friendship they shared, but was quickly brought back to the woman in his arms. His love for his wife, Alexandra Phoenix, was anything but simple.

"As a matter of fact, Mr. Phoenix, wasn't it you who said you always wanted this smile of mine staring back at you?"

"Indeed it was, Mrs. Phoenix. Indeed it was," he said with satisfaction, carrying her, and her smile, into their stateroom.

I hope you enjoyed reading *Simple Pleasures* as much as I enjoyed writing it. I have a feeling this will not be the last time you see these characters. Alexandra and Joshua's story introduced us to Candice Carwin and Landon Phoenix. Look forward to finding out how their new friendship takes them on a journey neither wanted nor expected.

Sincerely,

Natasha Simmons